Uncle Henry recognised the face without any difficulty. He agreed, with an inward shudder, that he did not wish to see more. At a police station he signed the necessary papers. There would have to be an inquest, which he must attend. But its verdict would almost certainly be accidental death. That was all for the moment, they told him, since there were no clothes or property to be handed over.

"Why not?" asked Mr. Frobisher, who had not gathered the full degradation of that drunken death.

"The body was naked when found. We have no idea where he entered the water. But we do know he was found some distance from where he drowned."

"Someone must have found his clothes," Uncle Henry protested. "Or been looking after them, more likely. Someone, a friend, I suppose, would surely have tried to get help when he disappeared in the water."

"No one did so."

Other titles in the Walker British Mystery Series

JOSEPHINE
BELL
Treachery in Type

WALKER AND COMPANY · NEW YORK

First published in the United States of America in 1980 by the
Walker Publishing Company, Inc.

This paperback edition first published in 1983

ISBN: 0-8027-3039-6

Library of Congress Catalog Card Number: 79-67548

Printed in the United States of America

10 9 8 7 6 5 4 3 2 1

I

The buzzer sounded on George Carr's desk.

"Yes?"

"Mrs. Grosshouse to see you, George."

"Who?"

"Mrs. Grosshouse, reception says. There's no appointment for her."

"Give me reception, Madge."

After a brief pause another female voice, higher, less articulate, said, "It's Mrs. Grosshouse, Mr. Carr." The voice sank to a whisper. "An old lady. Says she's been with us, with the firm, I mean, sir, for forty years. Insists—"

The voice died. George sat back, wildly flogging a memory that had never responded to violent treatment. He gave it up and tried unavailingly to get into touch again with Madge.

Then his door opened. Madge herself, flushed and fearful, appeared.

"Mrs. Grosshouse to see you, Mr. Carr."

A contralto voice from behind her said vigorously, "Anita to you, George. Anita Armstrong. Don't look at me with that blank stare. I don't expect you to remember my face. I'm an old woman but the name must be familiar, even if the works are out of print in this benighted country."

George pulled himself together. He had jumped to his

5

feet automatically when she appeared. He now advanced with outstretched hand. Certainly the name meant something. What the hell—?

"You must forgive my staff. Madge is my personal secretary, a very literate person, Mrs. Gross—Miss Armstrong. She knows the titles, don't you, Madge?"

"Of course, Mr. Carr."

Clearly this was an order, to be obeyed instantly. Madge was gone, closing the door softly behind her, before George Carr had installed his visitor in the comfortable chair on the other side of his desk and settled himself in his own opposite.

"I do apologise for the muddle below stairs," he began, but Anita Armstrong interrupted him.

'I wrote," she said, severely.

This was too much. George defended himself.

"We have had no letter. When did you write, Mrs. Grosshouse?"

"Three days ago with a first-class stamp."

"From?"

"Devon. Don't tell me you don't have my address?"

Clearly her own temper, already provoked, was rising and with it a return to the American way of speaking that the recent years in England had not altogether displaced.

The buzzer on his desk saved him. It was Madge again, with much needed information. Frantically he took this down, answering merely with 'yes' at intervals. When it was over he turned again to his uncomfortable intruder.

"Please forgive me. That was my secretary again to say your letter has been found and was put on one of the other directors' desk. He did not recognise the name Grosshouse as belonging to Anita Armstrong."

"Nor did you, George."

"I apologise."

They glared at each other. He was remembering a little now. A strong-faced, strident-voiced woman, much admired by his father, who had not been able to do much for her difficult novels until the late thirties, when she had suddenly produced a best-seller, vindicating the old boy's stubbornly held opinion. What was the title again? He glanced down at the paper on his desk, the notes supplied by Madge. *Too Late for the Dawn Chorus.* It had sold over a hundred thousand in England alone.

He looked up again, with his professional smile replacing the puzzled frown.

"You always did put the wind up me," he said, frankly. She laughed.

"Nerves on my part, I expect," she answered, melting to that smile in which she recognised his father, long dead. "Besides, you'd only just joined him. Didn't know if you were coming or going. Very high-brow, too. Thought it was a proof of mediocrity to sell well."

She laughed again and added, "You don't seem to have changed much. Look pretty much the same except you've got rid of the moustache and moved it out to sideburns and let the thatch grow. Thank God not further than the collar. Never knew it was *curly*! Men have all the luck!"

The ice seemed to be breaking. If Madge had managed by some miracle to find a copy of the old *Dawn Chorus* he could claw his way to the summit of this unlooked-for problem. Besides—

"If you can forgive me as my father would no doubt have implored you to do, will you tell me why you wanted to see me today."

She had been nursing her over-large handbag on her knee all this time. Now she put it on the floor beside her, pulled off her good, thick, leather gloves, unbuttoned her heavy tweed coat and sat back.

The story she had to tell covered the last thirty-five years. Though George dared not interrupt, he groaned inwardly at the delay to his other business. Once he pressed his buzzer for Madge, whispered 'coffee' into it, and when that

7

came placed a cup within reach of Anita Armstrong, who ignored it, while he sipped at his own, waiting for an interval into which he could force the only question for which he needed an answer. Which was, did she want her work revived? Reprinted? But until she came out of her long journey into the past and picked up the cup of cooling, rather revolting beverage, he must endure.

It was not an unusual tale; shorn of the over abundant detail it should not have taken more than half the time it did to relate. He whipped up his memory again, but with even less success than before. Had the novels been unduly verbose? Even if they had been compelling, as they must have been to succeed so astonishingly from 1938 until after the war.

After the war. Yes. The war. Those years when there was no petrol for pleasure-driving, no evening entertainment without braving the blackout and the bombs. No television, except for the wealthy. Such as Anita Armstrong and she was in America, apparently, where the restrictions—

He dragged his mind back to the present, to the large, tweed-upholstered figure in his comfortable clients' chair.

Miss Armstrong had met Louis Grosshouse in London in the Summer of 1939 during his usual visit to England on business. Each saw in the other, beside a mutual youthful attraction in the way of looks, minds and pleasure in the arts, an extended opportunity for increase in their separate businesses, or professions, as Anita preferred to describe them.

Louis Grosshouse, with American clear-eyed energy, also understood all the implications of the European political situation. He proposed marriage, Anita accepted and they were settled in his New York apartment flat, with a holiday home as well on Long Island, before the first moves of the 'phoney war' disappointed the news media of the world.

She was blissfully happy, Miss Armstrong told George,

8

but there were no children, only another four novels to carry on the success of *Too Late for the Dawn Chorus*.

"They did even better in the U.S." she explained. "Paper got very difficult here, I believe."

"Indeed it did," George told her, remembering those early years of the war in his father's former office after his own air-force training had been brought to an abrupt end by one of the first real air raids when he was on leave at home. A badly damaged knee grounded him for the duration. He often wished he had lost his leg altogether. An artificial one would have been more useful and less painful.

He had shared his father's frustrations, shared with the publishers over paper, printing, binding and other restrictions. How come he could not remember a thing about Anita Armstrong? Too highbrow? Surely not. Too bitter over his crippled state that kept him out of things? Truthfully, for he was an honest man, George reminded himself that he had been bloody thankful for it as the raids into Germany increased and with them the casualties.

"Paper," he told Miss Armstrong, "was worth its weight in gold. So the U.S. did you proud, did it? And yet," he went on, trying to push the story forward towards the present time, "you gave up writing, didn't you?"

"When Louis was killed, my talent, such as it was, died too."

She said it magnificently, proudly, as she must always have said it, George thought, beginning to admire his visitor, even to fear for her, as a vulnerable 'revenant'.

"He insisted upon joining the armed forces," Miss Armstrong went on, still in the tone that befitted a saga. "He was well over forty, but very fit. He was killed in the landings in Italy."

"I'm sorry," George said, meaning it, bowing his head a little. "But then?"

Mrs. Grosshouse was off again. Her life in Long Island,

without Louis, without the books, without the literary background or his business friends.

"They drop you pretty quick out there when you stop publishing," she said. "My local friends were fine, but the New York crowd just faded away."

That would also happen in England, George told himself. Her loss, too, would soon be forgotten or simply merge with the much greater, more immediately understood holocaust. Nowadays, too, for Americans, the generous heroism that had destroyed Louis Grosshouse would not be admired. Vietnam had soured the taste of glory, fouled with cynicism the beauty of sacrifice.

He glanced at the fatally delayed letter on his wide desk. She had noticed his break in the attention he was giving her and had reached for her cold coffee. He snatched at the opportunity.

"May I ask? Is this a visit? Devonshire? The house in Long Island—?"

"Good God!" she answered irritably. "Surely you've gathered by now I left the States *years* ago? *Years!* Actually in 1953. You must have been in the firm by then, even if Fred didn't see fit to present you. I should think he'd have told you."

"Of course he did."

Red-faced, George was at last remembering. His father, the Frederick Carr of the firm's title, sixty by then, had said, "You've missed something, my boy. The famous Anita Armstrong, best-seller of war time. Came to tell me she was a widow, had left New York for Devon and would never write again."

And it had made no impression on him at all, not even to the point of reading the best-seller. No wonder! *Too Late for the Dawn Chorus*. A bloody sight too late.

"You must forgive me, Miss Armstrong. No excuse, really."

She said, with unexpected gentleness, "Of course I do.

10

It's been a long time. You were a young man then, still suffering from that knee injury—"

They looked at each other, each astonished by the sudden understanding.

"I've taken up far too much of your time, Mr. Carr."

"George."

"Far too much, George. And not even come to the point yet. Which is that I've begun to write a new novel and I want to know how I stand about it. There!"

George was astonished. It was the last thing he expected. During the long tale of her American experiences he had let his thoughts wander to vague memories of those thirties novels that he had managed to avoid reading in spite of his father's warning that she was going to pull off a best-seller and even vaguer speculation about how he was to revive them or rather it, the best-seller. But a *new* one, at this interval in time!

"A *new* one," he said. "A new *novel*," and stared at her, completely at a loss.

She laughed, with childish pleasure and abandon, no malice, no resentment. Then she picked up her large handbag and got to her feet.

"You are flabbergasted," she said, holding out her hand across the desk, where George in turn was struggling from his chair.

"I've done the first four chapters and I know how to go on from there. What I want you to find out is how I stand with Haseldyne. Is Ian Macalister still with them? I haven't had the nerve to inquire. He was very helpful before the war, but young. I suppose he did survive?"

"Very much so. He's still there. Chairman of the directors."

She nodded.

"Good. Tell him I've not gone out of my mind, won't you?"

There could be no immediate answer to this so George

11

shook the outstretched hand, sprang to the door and guided Miss Armstrong to the lift that bore her down to the street. As he turned away he heard the buzzer on his desk calling him back to work.

One interview, with a patient novice, dreading to hear the worst, not even understanding that a personal summons must mean at least one foot fixed on the ladder of fame. The young man, both dazed and emotional, gave no trouble, for he agreed with everything George told him and left to celebrate his pathetic little success with a beer and a sandwich at the nearest pub.

No lunch engagement, thank God, George told himself. He could not have faced another author that morning. But he must see the results of Madge's research and then try to get in touch with Ian Macalister. No, try for Haseldyne first. Worth a lunch, perhaps? Feeling reckless, he put through a call and was lucky enough to find the Chairman in person.

He said, "Do you remember a writer called Anita Armstrong?"

"*Too Late for the Dawn Chorus.* 1937 or 8. Pre-war, anyhow. Did very well till she deserted in the war."

"Deserted?"

"Married a Yank and ran off to New York when the balloon went up. Two or three follow-up novels, not so popular here. What about her? I thought she was dead?"

"By no means. A widow since 1943, been living in Devonshire since 1953 and is writing a new novel."

"The devil she is! How do you know?"

"She's been here. Just told me. I wondered if you'd be interested."

There was no immediate reply. After a few seconds George went on, "She says she's written the first four chapters. Wants to know if I think I can place it. Mentioned your name, but says she wanted me to know first. I haven't checked yet but I seem to remember—"

"That she has an unfinished contract with us. You'd remember that if you forgot your own name, George."

"I certainly forgot hers. Look, are you free today? Now, for instance? Have a bite of lunch?"

"Where?" asked Ian Macalister, cautiously.

"The usual do you?"

"Fine. In half an hour. I'll check on that contract."

"So will I. But I think you ought to see her."

"I wonder. Seeing you."

Macalister rang off and sat for several minutes considering. A tricky situation, perhaps. Why, she must be all of seventy. Check that contract himself. Avoid gossip at present. If he had to take the new book it would have the best chance if he put it out as a surprise, more than that, a bombshell. And reprint *Dawn Chorus* he groaned.

His phone rang.

"A Mr. Cassell would like to speak to you, sir."

"Apologies. I have just left for a lunch appointment."

"Very good, sir."

Ian Macalister spoke briefly to his personal secretary, suggesting a line of research similar to that George had laid down for Madge.

What an amazing thing! Anita Armstrong. Unbelievable, really.

II

Mrs. Grosshouse left her agent's offices feeling decidedly shaken by her reception there. Not that George had been rude to her; far from it. He had been falling over himself trying to place her correctly, both in his memory and in the present day. It was the astonishing width of the gap that had upset her at the time and continued to do so all the way back by Underground to her hotel. She would have preferred the open air, though far from fresh. But she dared not attempt the buses of today. Many of the numbers on them were familiar, but their routes were not, for these had been twisted and confined, by one-way sections and forbidden turns, into a maze where remembered landmarks were replaced by concrete towers. Quiet squares with their central private gardens destroyed had given place to clusters of mean bungalows, while fresh destruction was hidden behind hoardings plastered with hideously insistent advertisements.

Still feeling shaken, Mrs. Grosshouse consulted her hotel about a possible train home that afternoon. There really was no point in staying. Her publisher might no longer be the old Haseldyne in spirit, even though Ian was on the board of directors. Ian Macalister, as an enthusiastic young man in his early years with the firm had been her friend and supporter from the beginning. As her admirer when she reached best-seller status he had been willing to obey her slightest wish. After she stopped writing he had, for several years, implored her to begin again. But the correspondence had died, from her own fault, she suddenly acknowledged and wept bitterly.

She was not overcome, however, by this extreme of self-indulgent regret and remorse until after she had arrived back at her small, pretty home in Siddicombe, a village scarcely more than a hamlet, near an arm of the spreading harbour that lay beside and behind the much larger village of Salcombe. A narrow road beside the creek led to the ferry across the harbour to Salcombe itself.

Perhaps it was the absence of her excellent daily house-keeper, Mrs. Droge, to welcome her with an early dinner and the comfort of hearing local gossip. But Mrs. Droge was on holiday for a week, told to amuse herself for seven days while Mrs. Grosshouse attended to her business affairs in London. That was what she had said and it was this gesture that had implied her secret expectations, that had rendered their shrivelled reality so bitter, all this that had brought on those tears of disappointment and self-pity.

Later, with characteristic resilience, she told herself that it would do her good to cook and do for herself for three days before Mrs. Droge arrived home.

By the next morning the London visit and its outcome had shrunk to their true proportions and Mrs. Grosshouse was able to buy a small amount of refrigerated food at the village shop and explain as shortly and vaguely to the various acquaintances she came across that her business calls had been shorter than she expected and for the rest London had become quite unbearable.

Most of those she spoke to had not visited the capital for several years, or indeed, ever. But their children, now almost grown-up, had done so and brought back very different reports, mostly favourable, often glowing. So they did not dispute their old neighbour's verdict but decided to wait until Mrs. Droge was back, for there was nothing the

15

housekeeper did not know and was not slow in telling about her ageing, perhaps now failing mistress. This was quite routine, for Mrs. Grosshouse herself had never talked to anyone, certainly would never have talked to Mrs. Droge, about her early career as an author.

But there was nothing failing about Anita Armstrong. Though her conversation with George Carr had been inconclusive, very upsetting in its way, it had been, she found later, most powerfully invigorating. Simply to recall her past glories had, upon reflection, gone far to demolish the heavy weight of the intervening years. As soon as she was back in her cottage, Anita dumped her shopping on the kitchen table and went to her workroom, small but south-facing, where her notes for the new novel lay spread out where she had left them the night before. She smiled grimly to think that she had flown to this, her unborn child, for comfort, and found the poor little thing still living, quietly developing in fact, as a foetus should, for having been conceived it needed from her only nourishment.

She had taken these sheets from their locked drawer last night, but not only for comfort. Perhaps she had intended to destroy them. Not now. What did it matter if George was doubtful, if Ian at Haseldyne was not interested. The novel was coming alive quite as fast as they always did, always had done. New characters were appearing, distant but distinct, approaching steadily to take their places in a story that had widened and deepened already this morning.

When Anita had added to her notes once again, shaken and sorted her plot, she arranged it about the overall theme of her story to give her a beginning that, she hoped would at once engage the reader. She then took another sheet of paper, headed it Chapter V in the true old-fashioned style and plunged into the now flowing stream of her tale.

The heap of pages, written in longhand, in pencil, grew beside her on the table until Mrs. Grosshouse, looking at her watch at last, discovered that it was after two and knew that she was both tired and uncommonly hungry.

Country air again and handwork she told herself smugly, but was dismayed to realise she would have to prepare her own lunch. She compromised with bread and cheese, an apple and coffee and went back to work at three, knowing she would be obliged to cook a real meal in the evening or she would not be able to keep going at the new, rejuvenated pace.

However, she was spared the effort in the kitchen, for a friend in Salcombe, Sarah Haston, rang up to ask her to come to them for supper.

"We've got the Fords coming," Sarah told her, "Joan saw you leaving the Post Office this morning and was surprised you were back so early. Nothing wrong, I hope?"

"Certainly not," Anita answered. "Thank you. I'd like to come. I'll tell you when I see you."

She rang off. It was always annoying to be interrupted, but in this case the outcome was pure gain. Her spirits rose. She went on writing. The pile of sheets grew.

At five she looked at her watch again. The scene at which she was looking as she wrote began to grow dim; the people who moved and talked, felt and thought all about her while she dived into first one character then another as the story line directed, now left her, fading away, vanishing without trace, folding back perhaps into that part of her own mind and heart that had originally split them off, brought them out as separate entities.

She sighed a little, feeling her former exhaustion return, augmented. But she gathered together her loose sheets, nine of them, put her notes on top with the pencil and the india-rubber and left the whole collection out on her desk. Locking up was for visits away from home. She did not fear robbers or vandals in Siddicombe. The harbour was a good barrier as far as Salcombe toughs were concerned. And Salcombe was a far more attractive target for strangers.

Sitting down with her elderly friends to a well-chosen, delicious meal in the dining room of Professor Haston's house below Bolt Head was, Anita decided, the most pleasant and satisfying thing she had known since she started for London four days ago.

"I think my journey was a mistake," she said. "I don't suppose I could have guessed, certainly not known, what London is like now. All the same—"

Professor Haston broke in.

"But Anita, known *what*? You didn't tell us you *were* going or *when* or even *where*! Mrs. Droge rang me up, me not Sarah, to ask me what you were up to, because you had simply told her 'on business' with absolutely no detail."

"Because I wasn't sure," Anita answered.

"Not sure of *what*?"

"Don't badger me, Mervyn."

The vicar said gently, "I expect you've forgotten, but a few months ago, I think it was when we had snow in early January, you said quite suddenly, in the church porch, after early service, 'If this goes on I shall take to writing again—' "

"Or something equally desperate," she added, with a laugh. "Well, that's exactly what I did. And am continuing to do."

"Well," said Sarah. "No one else could add anything to that."

Anita went on to give them a detached, cynical account of her conversation with George Carr, the charming young admirer turned careful chairman of his company. They were indignant on her behalf. The vicar, who had read none of her works, but knew her simply as an ageing woman who had been notorious, if not well-known, in literature, already felt her return to it was dubious, though his wife, Joan, was plunged into confusion. At the hospital where she had been a V.A.D. for the war there had been no time to read books, though the patients were always asking for

18

them. Especially the popular kind her own family did not approve of.

"How marvellous," she said breathlessly and could not go on because Geoffrey was frowning and Mervyn had the wicked look in his eye that he always turned on her poor attempts to state more than she knew.

"That's as may be," Anita greeted her response in her direct tone, but then repented. "When I came here to settle," she explained, "I meant never to let people find out who I really was."

"But you *are* Mrs. Grosshouse?" the vicar interrupted anxiously.

"Of course, but that wasn't very real any more, with Louis dead in Italy. Anyway nobody realised who I was as well, until Mervyn and Sarah retired and then only a few people around Salcombe."

There was a break in the conversation about London until they had moved into the Haston sitting room with its wide view down the harbour entrance, Bolt Head rising to the right, beyond the little deceptive bay that had lured the drunken crew of the *Hertzogovin Sicilie* to put her ashore on the rocks in tea-clipper days.

As usual, over coffee, they discussed lightly the shipping, the moorings, the yachts, the inevitable summer over-crowding, the activities on the water of their respective young. Anita listened, but since she lived alone at Siddicombe and had no relations, even Armstrong ones, in England, she had nothing to contribute.

The vicar and his wife left early. When they had gone and she herself had been persuaded to stay for a while, Mervyn Haston said, "Will you tell us exactly *why* you have started writing a new book? A novel, is it?"

"Semi-historical. Edwardian era. I know it. I was born into it."

"An urge, then, because the writers of today make such an unholy mess of it when they try to use it?"

19

"No, Mervyn. Nothing so literary. Money. Pure and simple."

Sarah exclaimed, "But we always thought you were rolling."

"So did I, until recently. But the demand slowly slipped away and the paperbacks ran out here and then in the States. Oh yes, Louis invested my money very carefully and successfully, but I suppose I ought to have gone and lived abroad when he died, not come here where the taxes skin you to the bone."

"So you actually feel you have to start earning your living all over again," Mervyn said slowly.

"That's exactly it. And I've started up not really knowing if my old contract still works or if even George Carr, let alone my publisher, is ready to work for me."

She paused, lost her angry expression as a beaming smile broke out all over her face.

"I think it's all right," she said, nodding happily. "I feel it might work like *Dawn Chorus* all over again."

For the rest of the week the new story moved forward rapidly. Two chapters were added in their initial draft and after some fresh development, written in the form of short notes, had been worked into them to follow the overall line of the plot, chapter six reached its designed crises by the afternoon of Mrs. Droge's return.

The housekeeper had been warned that she would find her mistress already back from London. Mrs. Droge had not been very far away, as she had a married niece at Wembury, further down the coast. It had been a nice opportunity to visit her; too short a holiday for going further afield. Besides, she had already booked her summer holiday in Spain with her brother and sister-in-law from Plymouth. At Wembury she had been told by telephone, that Mrs. Grosshouse was back, in one of her moods, apparently, according to Phyllis at the Post Office shop in Siddicombe.

So when she had let herself into the small house with her own key, Mrs. Droge was not surprised to hear no sound, not even when she knocked gently at the sitting-room door. Having her afternoon nap, the housekeeper decided, moving on into the kitchen.

She glanced through the window into the garden, peaceful in the late afternoon sun. Still weedy, she noticed. Nothing done there yet, in spite of all the complaints about having no time before going off to London, about how tiring it was now she had begun feeling her age. Not as old by half as poor old Harry, who did manage to grow her a few vegetables beyond the gooseberry bushes. He wasn't going to keep coming for ever, without he got a bit of encouragement now and again. But she wasn't going to get caught in on it, herself, not she.

Turning away from the garden Mrs. Droge filled the kettle and put it on the stove, then quite mechanically began to assemble crocks on the trolley, with a plate of biscuits and a small jug of milk, all ready to wheel in to Mrs. Grosshouse when the tea was made.

A noise overhead startled her. A thump, as if something heavy had fallen on the floor, followed by a series of smaller thumps. Silence, then clear, unmistakable.

"Damn!" Miss Armstrong said, in her strong contralto, clambering away from the chair she had been sitting on to pick up the dictionary she had let slip to the ground. "Damnation! Half-past five and I've got to get my own tea!"

Mrs. Droge, grim-faced, for she hated swearing, especially in ladies of a certain age and she had heard every word spoken aloud above stairs, seized the handle of the trolley to push it out into the little hall, but was checked by the scream of the kettle as it reached the boil.

She went to deal with it. As she expected the kettle's signal had also reached her mistress's understanding. The latter clattered downstairs, opened the kitchen door and said, "Thank God you're back! I've been on my own for three days. Misery!" She pulled herself up. "Hope you had a good time. I didn't try to get you back early, though I needed you, but *badly*!"

"Thank you," Mrs, Droge said. "It was very pleasant at Wembury."

She did not explain that she would not have broken the holiday for any reason or appeal, outside illness. Not from Mrs. Grosshouse.

She had now finished filling the two small teapots. She put one on the trolley.

"Well let's get on with the tea," Anita said, turning away, leaving the trolley to her housekeeper. As they went in procession to the sitting room she said over her shoulder, "I did remember to get you a loaf, Mrs. Droge. And there's a small joint in the fridge for tonight. But I've not done any real shopping as I've been—"

She stopped. This wouldn't do. Nobody must know yet what she was doing. Not until—

"I took the liberty of making a few purchases in Plymouth before I left," Mrs. Droge said, formally. "My niece and me was in there shopping this morning. Tom gave me a lift from the station on his motorbike."

"Pillion?" asked Mrs. Grosshouse, enthralled.

"No, madam. He has a sidecar. For his family."

Mrs. Droge was shocked. She made for the door with a set face.

"That was very thoughtful of you," Mrs. Grosshouse said, hastening to make amends. "What should I do without you?"

"I don't know, I'm sure," Mrs. Droge answered, only half soothed.

III

Chapter seven of the new novel was begun and going forward without any break in its rapid progress when George Carr's letter arrived. It had been favoured with a first-class stamp, but nevertheless had taken five days to reach Siddicombe. The contents sobered her.

A fairly long letter. Careful explanation, neutral conclusions.

"They sound as if I was a high-powered bomb they were trying to defuse," Anita snorted aloud. "All the same—"

She read it a second time. All the same Ian Macalister had not forgotten her, not in the least. He remembered far more than George had done. Well, you could expect that, he was older and he had been her personal editor in those far distant days. The old original Haseldyne had been alive still, hadn't he? He hadn't liked *Dawn Chorus* until her sales had gone beyond the ten thousand mark. But he hadn't given her the V.I.P. treatment till they topped fifty thousand.

She went back to the letter. George assured her that there certainly was one book left in her old contract. Ian agreed that this was so, but did not think it was enforceable. However, for the sake of old times he was fully prepared to honour it provided the new work measured up to modern taste. Whatever he may mean by that, George wrote, cover-

23

ing himself in advance by putting the publisher's remark in quotation marks.

Anita Armstrong knew what Ian meant. He wanted to feel he would not be a fool to publish an old woman's swan-song in case it should turn out to be pure rubbish and a flop. Her work had been very popular in its time, but after so long a gap would it still be popular?

In her heart she knew he was right. But she also knew she could do it. She had not been asleep all those years. Her eyes and ears had been as acute as before during all that time in America when she had been blissfully happy. Even when she was terrified, and later with her slain heart too numbed consciously to listen or watch. Not until she found this quiet home back in England, among people who took their lives as they came and did not ask many questions or just the very few that the television did not answer more or less intelligibly. Here in Siddicombe she gradually understood that she had never really stopped seeing and listening. She was ready once more to turn her knowledge, her observation into words and stories about people.

She looked at the letter again. George encouraged her to continue writing her new book. Mr. Macalister did not like to demand it, but he had gathered that the great man was anxious to deal with the work himself, if only for old time's sake and would be most grateful if she could see her way to letting him have a look at the first few chapters, even if in an early draft. Perhaps if she agreed to this she would have lunch with Mr. Macalister in London, taking the manuscript with her, when they could discuss the whole project.

It was humiliating, but she submitted. Only this time she would stay for one night only in horrible London and Mrs. Droge would be at home to greet her when she got back.

Five chapters, she decided, should be enough to convince Ian one way or the other. But on re-reading she decided that seven would look better. So she would finish the one

24

she was half-way through. And then she must type a rough draft of the seven to take with her to London.

She made two carbon copies; one to send to George, because he was, after all, her agent and would expect it; one to keep for herself, perhaps to revise later. She delivered her agent's copy of the seven chapters by hand to the Carr offices, with a note for George expressing guarded approval of his programme for her and explaining that she was on her way to lunch with Mr. Macalister who would no doubt be in touch with him, George, later.

As she expected, Ian did recognise her. He had always regretted the break in her writing, he told her. He was delighted to know she had begun again. It was just that the market was in a very difficult state with the economy in such a mess—

"No, Ian," Mrs. Grosshouse interrupted, "you know perfectly well how to manage the economy. Didn't they give you a gong for services to export? You're simply worried that I may be past it. Aren't you?"

He laughed. It was the old Anita. Not changed an atom. Always did run herself down, the awkward old masochist. Treasured the scornful notices more than the treacle.

"All right, Anita," he agreed. "Pull up the drawbridge. Man the walls. Seriously, have you honestly never written anything since you came home from the States?"

"Home!" she exclaimed, suddenly broken by that word. She went on in a very different, softened tone, "My home was there until Louis never came back to it."

She did not answer his question which had in any case been an idle one. After a long silence he began to tell her, with a very professional air, about Haseldyne's present position in the publishing world. Their fiction section was smaller than it had been, very selective for straight novels, but not exclusive, not highbrow.

"You still avoid the high-brow pornography, do you?" Anita asked, her old manner restored. "And the deeper

25

mud of the sub-conscious? I try to keep up with it, but the public library in Plymouth is slow. Not its fault, too many retired professionals who can't afford to buy books. I can't afford the bus fare to go there very often, nor the car park fee if I drive in."

"We have a flourishing thriller section now," Ian told her. "Adventure, crime, spy stories. The biggest of the best-sellers come in that sort of thing, as I expect you know."

"I have noticed it," she told him. "They are going back in history too, to find new backgrounds, aren't they? Mine is set at the turn of the century, because I was an Edwardian child. But it is not a thriller and I doubt very much a best-seller."

"I can't wait to read it," Ian told her, meaning every word.

The book gathered momentum. Pages flowed in longhand much as they always had done. But the typewriter lay covered on its table, untouched since Anita's return from her second visit to London. It was not that she disliked typing, though she had never been able to put down her stories direct in type from their creation in her mind. The trouble was that now she found the act of working the machine quite tiring after half an hour, exhausting if she tried to continue further. Moreover this excess of fatigue spoiled the flow of her narrative. She found herself considering how to cut down description or dialogue to save herself typing labour. This was madness she rightly decided. She would have to get the work done for her and put up with the expense. It was a gamble. But wasn't the whole project a gamble? A desperate plan to keep the house and Mrs. Droge, to stay in Siddicombe, to escape the final solution, an old people's home.

A few days of pause, with feverish searching of advertisements, brought her to a state of desperate calm. Professional typists, only names in directories, were dangerous and expensive. She dared not attempt to use them when they would have to type from her longhand, sole copy of her work. She considered her neighbours, her friends and acquaintances. She was ashamed to realise how little she really knew about them and their activities.

So when, seeking to amend her ways, she met Mrs. Ford, the vicar's wife, at the local Post Office shop she did not smile politely and pass by, but stopped to say a few words to her about how interesting Mervyn Haston had been the other evening at supper in Salcombe.

"Yes, indeed," Mrs. Ford answered, and looking about her said, "I have Kate home for a few days, Mrs. Grosshouse. Oh, there you are, Kate. We were speaking about the Hastons. You've seen them quite lately, haven't you?"

"I thought you were in Plymouth," Anita said, looking at the smiling girl who had collected various packets and cartons from that part of the Post Office that formed a general store.

"So I am. But we have this break over Whitsun and Professor Haston wanted some typing done, so I've been going over to Salcombe every morning since I came home."

"Secretarial!" Anita was surprised. "I thought you were studying art of some kind?"

This was pure invention, for she had never considered Kate's activities at all and had been barely conscious of her existence, though she had seen the girl about from early childhood. Children had never occupied her attention much, having none of her own, nor feeling the need of them.

"Commercial art and design," Kate answered, still smiling at the funny old woman who had frightened her once or twice in the past by calling to her as she passed the little dark house in the lane on her way to the village school.

"But you can type?"

"Well, yes."

"Does Mervyn want you for long?"

"I don't know. It's an article for the university press."

"From longhand?"

"Oh, no. He does his own as a rule, straight on the typewriter, I think. But he needs a lot of carbons for the article."

The Fords were turning away, mother and daughter inclined to resent this rapid fire of questions. Mrs. Grosshouse moved with them.

"You mustn't mind my asking all this," she said, breathing rather fast, "I want some typing done myself. I do type, but it tires me. I'm getting old, you know."

They knew and they showed that they did. But they stood still, patient as befitted vicarage people.

"You wouldn't be able to help me, I suppose?" Anita went on. "Naturally I would consider it professionally. I mean I would pay the going-rate."

The Fords exchanged glances.

"Mervyn gives her a pound a thousand words," Mrs. Ford said, stiffly.

"Whatever's right," Mrs. Grosshouse mumbled, Then, finding the conversation unbearable, she looked at her watch, exclaimed, "Good heavens, is that the time!" and rushed towards the door, only checking her flight as she reached it for she had not yet collected the goods she had gone there to find.

"If you can help me, Kate," she said, as she passed the Fords again. "Come in this evening and I'll explain."

Kate went to the cottage reluctantly, but encouraged by her parents, who reminded her of her duty to the old and infirm, however unreasonable their demands.

And unreasonable old Mrs. Grosshouse turned out to be. Kate came back to the vicarage not knowing whether to be angry or laugh.

"She says she's writing a book! A novel! At her age!"

The vicar said gently, "We've always thought her rather eccentric, haven't we? And living quite alone—"

"She's got Mrs. Droge."

"Not living in. Daily, only. It must make a difference, every night alone," Mrs. Ford added.

"All the same, writing what she calls a novel. She's actually typed some of it, but she says it makes her shoulder ache and takes up too much time because she types very slowly."

"Did you offer to help her?" Mr. Ford asked.

"In a way."

"Good girl."

"Well, I said I'd only done part of a commercial course and didn't have much spare time, so I couldn't really take it on, but I'd ask round at the college and see if I could find anyone. She's prepared to pay. You heard her say that, Mother."

"I wonder she can afford it," Mrs. Ford said, thoughtfully. "The village people seem to think she may be rather badly off now. Mrs. Droge's accounts of what goes on, I expect."

"How d'you mean?"

"Not getting repairs done in the house. Not as much food in the freezer."

"Has she got a freezer?" Kate was surprised.

"Oh, yes. She seemed to be very well off when she came here. Much better off than we were, don't you agree, Geoffrey?"

The vicar laughed.

"She'd been here quite a time when I got the curacy here and for All Saints. But yes, the village called her the rich American widow."

"I bet they didn't put it as politely as that," Kate told him.

"Never mind. We must try to oblige her. And we did see her at the Hastons not long ago. Don't you remember, Joan? She spoke about writing a book. The Hastons were not at all surprised."

29

"I was," said Mrs. Ford.

"Do your best to find her a typist, Kate, won't you?" the vicar urged.

"All right, Daddy, I will."

The next morning, alone in the house, with the vicar out on his rounds and Kate away to her college, Mrs. Ford rang up her friends, the Hastons. She found Sarah at home and explained Kate's problem. Mrs. Grosshouse was not easy to put off when she got an idea in her head, as Geoffrey knew only too well over church matters.

"I thought she was an atheist," Sarah Haston said.

"Not so simple. Calls herself agnostic, but does come to church quite often and wants to argue with poor Geoffrey."

"But Joan, isn't that what all the young are doing now?"

"They are indeed."

Sarah Haston had no wish to discuss religion with her friend. Besides, she was excited by her news. She said, firmly "Never mind about Anita's religion, Joan. She told us she was starting to write again, didn't she? She's going on seriously, then?"

"I suppose so. What did she write? When?"

"Ages ago. Before the war. She was quite well known. Did you never read *Too Late for the Dawn Chorus*? It made a sensation at the time."

"No. Never heard of it. I'm sure I never did."

"You ought to. It must still be in the library."

"I'll look for it."

And so she did. But as Sarah had forgotten to mention that the author wrote under her maiden name of Armstrong and Mrs. Ford could not find it under Grosshouse and as the very young librarian she asked had never heard the title, she did not find the book and continued to believe that her husband's rather overbearing parishioner was indulging in a senile extravagance that must be humoured if possible. And that the Hastons were always very excited about books of any kind.

In the meantime Kate, who was a good-natured girl, if not very intelligent, had been asking round among her contemporaries at the college and had been recommended to try a second-year student in the Design section, who was known to be ambitious and also usually hard up.

"Spends more than her allowance all the time," the recommender reported. "Do anything to make a bit on the side. Not that she needs a job like typing with *her* face and figure."

Judy Smith, Kate decided, ought to need very little effort to supplement her allowance in order to provide herself with all the parties, outings and amusements she needed. She had large deep blue eyes, high cheek bones, a wide full-lipped mouth, a smooth pale complexion and thick, gently curving corn-coloured hair. She was beautiful, well aware of it, but not blatantly conceited. To Kate's intense surprise and rather anxious pleasure, Judy accepted the offer of an unusual job.

"You mustn't mind what she says," Kate explained. "My father thinks she's a lonely soul with not enough to do. She disapproves of good works, or says she does."

"I don't mind what anyone says, if they come up with the lolly," Judy answered, smiling.

Kate, slightly shaken, reported success to Mrs. Grosshouse, but not her qualms. The writer would not have been interested if she had done so. She needed a typist; she was professional herself; she expected to employ a professional.

Nevertheless she took certain precautions over her manuscript. The longhand sheets of those first chapters that she had taken to Ian Macalister personally she locked away in a drawer of her desk. She would keep all the pencil drafts, she decided. She had been told that authors made money by selling such things. This novel might be worth curiosity, even historical value. But she would have to keep out her personal carbon copies of those first chapters to show the typist how she liked her work to be presented. There were rules, Ian had told her, but she was not to be guided by new rules at her time of life. This girl, Judy, would follow the rules she herself laid down.

Which she did. Mrs. Grosshouse found Judy willing, obedient, careful and accurate, if rather slow. But the girl came to her in the late afternoon, three times a week, after working at the college in Plymouth all the earlier hours of those days.

She wanted to have her wages weekly and calculated by the hour rather than by the usual thousand words. Mrs. Grosshouse agreed to this, being doubtful of her own counting ability and to avoid argument. At Mrs. Droge's suggestion she gave the girl an afternoon tea when she arrived and so avoided having to offer her a share of her own and her housekeeper's modest, but much more expensive, supper.

The system worked, the book went forward. After another visit to Haseldyne with five more chapters, Ian Macalister became more cordial, even taking Anita for lunch at the women's annexe of his club. As she said to Mervyn Haston, when he and Sarah came to a Sunday meal at the cottage, "If this goes on it'll be the Ritz before it goes to the printer."

IV

As for Judy, she found the typing a distinct bore. Not only was the old biddy's handwriting quite hard to read, but, she told her friends, she used a lot of words Judy had never seen before. That was bad enough, but when the Grosshouse complained that she had got them wrong she actually threw the dictionary at her and stood over her while she looked them up.

"Surely you don't stand for that?" her friends asked.

Judy simply smiled and repeated, "I need the lolly."

When they asked her if the stuff she was typing was worth it, apart from the money, she said it was some sort of a story about a girl who was bullied by her parents.

"Did she let them bully her?"

"No option. Years ago."

"Historical, you mean? Isn't that very old hat?"

"You're telling me! You should see the Grosshouse. She's out of the ark herself."

After a time her friends stopped asking Judy about the book she was typing. But their questions had stirred her into paying more attention to her work, so that she took the trouble to read those early chapters that had been typed by the author herself and upon which she had been told to model her own efforts. So that she found, to her surprise, that her employer had invented the beginning of a tale that held her attention and even induced her to read again her own carbon copies.

Mrs. Grosshouse took away the finished top copies. Judy did not know what she did with them and did not care. Her salary, based on hours of work, not words typed, was paid regularly every Friday.

When this arrangement had been going on smoothly for five weeks Judy's boy-friend, Chris Trotter, asked her to go with him to a party in Plymouth. It was to take place on the College premises, but was by subscription, to cover the hire of the hall and its adjoining kitchen. It was open to all members of the college and entertainments club, who could bring guests from outside, at double the members' subscription.

Chris wanted to bring two outside friends, he told Judy, but he would pay her subscription for her.

"Big of you," Judy said, "but I could afford it myself, really."

"You never!"

"Ya, honest. But I won't. I'll get something to wear instead."

Chris Trotter was still only a student, or he called himself such, though he was now twenty-nine. He had some talent, but he was lazy. He aimed at drawing for advertising. He already did a snazzy line in long-legged, rough-featured, but sharply dressed young men, hair curling down to their collars, none on their faces. He had admiring parents, or rather foster-parents, both of whom worked in a family business, so his personal allowance made him able to indulge himself to a degree unusual for his age and abilities. Not that he wasted time on any of the ordinary student vices. He did not abuse alcohol or drugs; he did not smoke. He owned a small car and he did quite an extensive research into the advertising industry, driving up to London for long weekends, visiting friends from the college who were working there now. He had managed in the course of the last year to make several new, reasonably prosperous friends with whom he could scrounge an occasional weekend bed in return for news of Plymouth, the college, the budding artists there, the potential talent for hire or exploitation. Feather, perhaps for his own future nest. He was a very plausible young man, attractive, charmingly countrified, as brightly smooth as an adder.

And now he had a girl-friend whose looks acclaimed his taste, even if her conversation palled. But he did not mind that. Usually he took her out in his car when the journey to some dive, discotheque or pub took up most of the time, eating and drinking or dancing, the rest. At the party in Plymouth to which he had invited her there would be dancing and a good sprinkling of strangers guaranteed to fall for her looks on sight. That would release him, when he needed to be free. Or so he hoped; so he planned. It ought to be easy enough.

Judy bought her dress in Exeter, at a boutique one of her girl friends recommended. It was a very shapeless affair in an artificial flimsy material like old-fashioned chiffon, but shinier; sea-green over a slightly more substantial, silky lining in sea-blue. It had sleeves like wings; it hung straight from a close neck trimmed with sparkling diamanté. In the shop it looked rather like an elaborate nightdress, falling in its rich folds from its coat-hanger. Except for the diamanté, so clearly not intended for bed.

Judy found it entrancing and the whole staff of the shop found Judy entrancing in it. By borrowing her next week's typing salary from the friend who was with her, added to her savings from two former weeks, she was able to pay for the dress in cash. She had to. It was not the kind of shop that gave credit to girls like Judy. The manager felt that girls with her advantages need never be insolvent.

The party was a great success. Judy and Chris made quite a sensation when they arrived, for they were a handsome couple. Judy's lovely face, set off in its blue-green floating frame, was matched by the changing lines of her exquisite figure, as they were revealed when she sat and moved

35

about. Chris felt genuine gratitude mixed with his admiration. Moreover, he did not have to wait long before he found himself forcibly excluded from the circle of eager males that surrounded her. Not all lads, either. Half amused, noticing grey, even white, heads bent towards her, he told himself he had better take care. He must not flaunt his prize too openly. Thick she might be in some ways, but she was quick enough when it came to the dough.

Waving a hand to Judy over the intervening heads, Chris went off to find Len Stockley. He had met the publisher twice already, the first time with friends in London, the second time, rather to his surprise, at the home of his foster parents, who lived near Minehead.

Somehow, from Stockley's voice and manner in London, he had not expected to find him at the home of people he himself knew as Aunt and Uncle Frobisher. But he welcomed the connection for it put him on the level in the way of background, a consideration that was most important to a climber. It set the seal upon some very delicate probing he had already made at home into the basic facts of his own orphaned state soon after birth.

Chris was quite open about his ambitions, both to himself and to any like-minded person. It was gratifying to find Len Stockley only a few rungs above him on the same ladder, starting from the same base of small provincial business. Chris's busy mind set to work at once to discover the meaning of the Frobisher connection and having guessed it readily devised a way of promoting his own interest further.

He found Stockley at the party without much trouble, because he rightly assumed the man would be fairly late in arriving, since he was coming alone. He expected him to hover near the entrances of the hall where the party was being held. He was right.

"There you are!" Chris exclaimed, moving purposefully through the clot of newcomers at the double doors. "Hope you've not been waiting long. Did you have a coat?"

Since the month of June was being its usual treacherous self this question was not really fatuous though Stockley stared as if he thought it was. But he only said, "No. Well, just a mac for the train."

"Fine. Then come to the bar and we'll find a drink."

"I thought you had a girl with you. You said—"

"Of course. She's been swallowed up in a ring of new admirers. I'll tell you a bit about this job of hers before we extricate her."

"Just as you like," Len said cautiously.

As he followed the young man whom he scarcely knew, he wondered, not for the first time, if the other's over cordial approach was due to innocence or guile. He hoped it was the former; common-sense and those friends where they had first met persuaded him to decide in favour of country-bred innocence. Still a student, hard-working and gifted by repute, enthusiastic for the arts as a whole. Surely there was no occasion for him to draw back, certainly not at this stage. And not forgetting for an instant his own position in the venture that threatened to crumble under him at the moment, particularly now that Clare, prime mover in setting it up, had threatened to walk out of it and out of his life at the same time.

"What's yours?" Chris asked his guest. The man looked positively sick, he thought. Was he in need of a fix? Surely not? Ned had told him Len Stockley was provided with all he should have. Part of the bargain? Ned had to agree. White, sweaty. He looked at him again. Up to a point that might be useful, but not with the interview with Judy coming up any minute now. Daren't risk him doing a bunk while he was fetching the kid.

"What are *you* having?" Stockley asked. "I'll have the same."

"Gin and bitter lemon," Chris told him, and gave the order.

"Tonic for me," Len corrected, "and ice."

"I'll get Judy," Chris said after the drinks arrived and he had paid for them. More than ever he felt this was a gamble. But a compelling one. Anyway, Judy was the king-pin of the ploy. Time to produce her and make the next move.

Gin had its usual restoring effect upon Len Stockley. Also the jab he had given himself before Chris found him. Those rational misgivings, so unlike his basic mild optimism, had already faded to a large degree before Chris returned with his girl friend. As she floated towards him in her spectacular dress, a knockout, a miracle, his spirits leapt up with as violent a movement as he made as he jumped from his stool at the bar.

"This is Miss Judith Smith," Chris said formally. "Mr. Leonard Stockley."

Judy giggled. She could not help it; her full name always made her laugh.

"Judy," she said, holding out her hand. "Chris likes to show off. You mustn't mind him, Mr. Stockley."

"Len," Stockley murmured. The lovely apparition's voice and manner had brought him back to earth with a thump. Wonderful to look at, but a real little provincial, of course. Student? Typist? His memory of what Chris had told him, never much considered, was now thoroughly confused, partly by gin, partly by unexpected feminine allure.

"They'll begin dancing any minute now," Chris said. "What say we find a quiet table where we shan't get sabotaged the whole time by couples charging past?"

"Good idea," Len agreed.

"I'll have to be able to get out myself," Judy protested. "I've got dates for dances."

"But we've got to tell—"

"I told them to find me. I expect they'll forget."

"You don't, you know," Chris told her. "You'd be bloody wild if they did. I'll tell them I booked you on the way here."

They both laughed, but stopped when they saw Stockley watching them. Chris led the way to a table in a corner of the hall far removed from the dance area. It was obvious from the presence of a hovering lad, dressed up as a waiter, that Chris had arranged this in advance. Not for him to muck in with the mob at the buffet help-yourself. The kid brother of a friend, a little bribe, a promise of one dance with the wonder-doll, what could be simpler? Of course one pair of hands couldn't manage four trays, so he'd have to join in when the queueing was nearly there. But that would leave Judy alone with Len. He could trust her to make a killing.

It all went perfectly as he had planned. Of course it did. He had a detailed account from Judy as they drove home after midnight.

Len Stockley was quite pleased when Chris beckoned to the young waiter, conferred with him in a low voice and then stood up.

"Time to get the eats unless we want to miss out on a choice."

He recited the menu and took the orders. Len looked amused. The young did themselves pretty well at these club parties, he knew. Heavily subsidised, of course. Their subscriptions were ludicrous for these days. When Chris and the youth moved away he turned to Judy.

"Are you a member here?" he asked.

"I'm a student in Art and Design, if that's what you mean," she answered.

"I meant this club? If it is a club party."

"I wouldn't know. Chris takes me about with him."

Baffling. Len tried again.

"You're a student but you do typing professionally, he tells me."

"For a poor old biddy who's writing a book. Ya, that's right."

"Tell me about it. She pays you, does she?"

"I wouldn't be doing it for fun. Not me."

It might have been for kindness, Len thought, but looking deep into the large blue eyes he did not find them clouded by any mist of sentiment. But he was still curious.

"Do you enjoy it? I mean is the writing interesting? Amusing? What is it, anyway?"

"She calls it a novel. It's a bit slow. Old-fashioned. It would have to be. She's over seventy, her Mrs. Droge says."

"Who is Mrs. Droge?"

"Does for her and that. Daily, eight to eight. Might as well live in, but has her own home, where she goes off in the afternoons. Not that she sees much of it with those hours. But she says she'd never find another if she lost it."

Stockley was not interested in Mrs. Grosshouse's domestic arrangements, but, prompted by Chris, he was interested in this book she was writing.

"Why do you think your Mrs. Grosshouse is writing a novel at her age?"

"Needs to cash in on something. Or so Mrs. Droge says. Seems to have lost money in the war and that."

"Does she know it isn't very easy to make money out of books?"

He spoke with a sudden bitterness in his voice that startled Judy. She was tired of talking about her employer and she was feeling hungry. She was looking across the hall, trying to see Chris when she spoke, but Len's acid statement made her turn to look at him. She was shocked by his sudden pallor and pinched mouth.

"Here," she protested. "What is this? Why all the questions? What's the point?"

"I'm a publisher," he said quietly, annoyed with himself for startling her. "I'm interested in authors, naturally."

"I never thought of Mrs. Grosshouse as an author."

"What would you call her then?"

40

"Just an old woman going a bit dotty. Humouring herself in a way."

"Look," said Len firmly. "How much has she actually written? Is it in chapters?"

"Well, yes. Nearly twelve of them. But I didn't start till after chapter seven. She'd done the first seven herself."

"So you don't know how the story began?"

"Oh yes, I do. She makes me type a top copy and two carbons from her longhand. She'd done the same for her own typing. So she started off by showing me a carbon of each of the seven chapters, so I could understand what it was about."

"Did you?" he smiled at her. "Understand the story I mean?"

Judy was affronted. Chiefly because she had asked herself precisely this question several times in the last five weeks.

"Of course," she said briefly, turning her gaze from him again and pleased to find Chris and that fancy-dress kid brother of Tom Lord making the slow, tortuous journey towards them between the close-packed tables.

The band started playing, couples moved out into the centre of the hall. At once conversation was impossible, for the noise of instruments and the beating of feet and hands tore at the ears and numbed the brains of spectators and performers alike.

None the less two of Judy's fresh admirers came to the table demanding their dances.

"So what?" she shouted, smiling from one to the other.

"So we take turns," they yelled back.

One of them snatched at the hand she lifted between them. The other flung an arm round her waist as she began to rise carefully from her chair. He found himself with a handful of gossamer nylon and fearful of tearing it let go as she swept away.

"Bad luck!" Len Stockley said, earning a very rude curse and a threatening scowl.

Left to himself he began to feel depressed but almost at once his young host arrived with two well-loaded trays, followed by the spurious waiter with two more. For economy's sake Len had not eaten since that morning. He greeted the appearance of the food with exclamations of pleasure.

"Starving, are you?" Chris asked, cheerfully, and when his guest nodded, his mouth already full, he grinned and went on. "What did you think of Judy?"

"Fantastic to look at."

"And this job of hers? Did you make anything of it?"

"Only that an old woman supplies her with longhand to make copies from, one top and two carbons. And she doesn't seem to know what the thing is, but I guess it must be a novel. Probably that novel every one seems to write in their youth and keep in the bottom drawer for the rest of their lives."

"I haven't," said Chris.

"No?" Stockley was not surprised, but he felt perhaps he ought to pretend he was.

Chris let that pass. He was not there, nor had he invited Len Stockley to this rather grotty do, in order to discuss his own career. He was learning how to cash in on his ability to draw for fashion. That would be his open career, his profession, his cover. He wanted Judy to make money too, share their mutual expenses. He had a plan, not part of the career building. Now was the time to approach it, while Judy was dancing away those two obligations she had fallen for. Kind-hearted, or just vain? Len was going on about Judy's typing.

"She almost made me feel I'd like to see this odd work. Will it be published, I wonder? Does the old woman—?"

"Mrs. Grosshouse. Widow of an American killed in the Second World War."

"American?"

"Not Grosshouse herself. English. Badly off now. It

might be a noble action on your part to offer to publish her."

"You must be joking?"

This was spoken with such weary bitterness that Chris was quite alarmed. Vague thoughts of commissions wilted in the bud.

Judy, having thrown off her two would-be followers, joined them and sat down, beaming healthily at the sight of her untouched tray of food.

In silence the two men watched her eat, until Chris judged she could be asked to use her limited powers of thought.

"Len and I were discussing this thing Mrs. Grosshouse is writing," he said. "Do you know what she means to do with it?"

"*Do*?" Judy asked, opening her big eyes very wide.

"Publish?" Len asked. "Does she want to see it in print? Have it published?"

"I don't know. Shall I ask her? I mean, you're a publisher, you said, didn't you? Would you do it for her?"

Again Stockley drew back in horror at any such idea. But Chris, quick on the ball, forestalled his impulse to refuse any part in such an idea.

"That isn't the way they work. Is it, Len? No good bringing the old lady into it at this stage. You'd have to see what she's written so far, wouldn't you, Len?"

The publisher agreed. He also decided that this party was going sour on him. When she had finished guzzling he'd get her to dance with him and then he'd be for the off. Young Chris Trotter was up to something and needed watching. From a distance, preferably.

Driving Judy home after midnight Chris said, "Another scalp in your belt, darling."

She answered, rather tartly, "I don't go for sugar-daddies, myself."

He laughed, partly at the old-fashioned phrase, chiefly

43

because he knew and guessed just how near the publisher was to the skids. No sugar for birds, there.

"He was interested in your work, too," he suggested.

"He asked a lot of questions."

"He told me he'd like to see what the old girl's done. Did he tell you that?"

"Hinted at it."

"Well, think it over, my pet."

"I could ask her if she'd mind," Judy said thoughtfully. She yawned. "God, I'm tired." She sank lower in her seat until her head rested against his left arm.

Chris moved her off gently and drove on in silence. Better drop the subject of Mrs. Grosshouse for the time being. But warn Judy when it next came up that on no account must she talk to her employer about Len Stockley. On the other hand he could put it to her that she would be doing the old girl a kindness to get the publisher interested. Yes, that would be the next move in the plan he had in mind. Plan? Fantastic dream, you nit, he told himself.

V

But Judy thought otherwise. She had not told Chris everything that had passed between herself and the publisher as
they danced together. To begin with she had not told Chris
that Len had danced a great deal better than either of the
two lads of her own age and college class. He might have
greying hair, this publisher, but he knew how to move and it
was a bit of luck the band was playing an old-fashioned
waltz and not any kind of jazz. He had held her close and
they could talk. He had explained how his business was
affected by the slump, but also by the lack of real talent in
the manuscripts offered to his firm.

"Nothing I'd dream of putting into print," he explained.
"Just plain porn, or dreary exercises in pseudo-psychology."

"What's that?" Judy asked. When he had given her some
sort of explanation she had added, "Well, it's nothing of
that. Just a girl of long ago, as they say, with a lousy father
who wants to keep her at home, and a wet mother who
keeps throwing the book of etiquette at her."

"Not very original. But you said just now that when you
first began your typing you were bored until the author
showed you her first few chapters. Why then? I mean, what
changed your mind?"

"Changed? I haven't changed. I just wanted to know
when she'd throw the parents over—this girl, I mean. Her
mum'd be easy. Dad's the problem. He's trying to marry

45

her off to a pal of his. Naturally she isn't having any."

Len was persistent.

"But there was something about those opening chapters that makes you put up with the slowness that follows?"

"It isn't exactly slow. Funny, sometimes, in a sarky kind of way."

"I'd really like to see those first chapters," Len told her, true enthusiasm as usual displacing the considerable doubts he had about Chris Trotter and his beautiful dumb floosie. He waited until he had danced her into a more complaisant frame of mind, then went on, "Couldn't you let me see some of the carbons?"

Judy was surprised. She had already lost the thread of their conversation. But retreat was usually the safest thing.

"Not really. She keeps them all. Locks them up, I wouldn't wonder."

"All three copies?"

"There aren't three copies. Not of those first seven chapters. I told you. She only let me see a carbon of each one, to put me what she called 'oh fay' with the story."

"And she's taken those carbons back, has she?"

Judy considered. End it here and now, as common-sense suggested. Or speak the whole truth for once? For what?

"If you still have them by you for reference couldn't you make a single copy of each—to show *me*?" Len continued, and to add to the attraction, "You could bring them up to my office in London, if you had time. I'd put up the return fare with pleasure."

A day in London. That tipped the balance, as he knew it would. Judy agreed.

"When?"

"At your convenience."

He took her out of the dance for a minute so that she could give him her home address on the back of an envelope he produced. He then tore off the front of the envelope to give to her. It had his office address in full, with the name of his firm, which was simply Leonard Stockley, publisher. He had added a telephone number which was not that of the firm.

"Write me a card or give me a ring to say when I can expect you," he said. "I'll let you know where to meet me."

The dance ended shortly after this. Neither of them referred to Mrs. Grosshouse again. The party broke up to go home soon after midnight.

Stockley went back to London by a very early morning train, after spending four uncomfortable hours at a railway station where neither bar nor buffet was open and the general waiting room stank of unwashed, sweaty humanity. The fact that he had not been able to afford an hotel bed for that night did nothing to lighten the profound gloom of his thoughts. Young Chris Trotter's bird had a lovely face and form and was well worth meeting. But it seemed very far from possible that any good in a business sense would come of it. He understood easily enough her total lack of any real education, even the smattering of the arts that gave young people of today an air, even an ill-used vocabulary, of culture. She had been totally vague about her elderly employer and also about the work on which she was employed by this Mrs. Grosshouse. An old woman's novel? More than likely the sort of rubbish he had to wade through every week. Not his readers' fault. They rejected more than half what came in without bothering him to endorse their decisions.

On the other hand his baser instincts found something in young Judy most compatible, most stimulating. Nothing emotional, nothing sexual. His passion could be more easily aroused and indulged, he knew, if he were not so desperately worried over his business venture. And it was in connection with the business that his hopes, coldly practical, were encouraged by that strong instinct for survival at any cost, by any means, that he knew was matched by a like quality in Judy. He thought he knew that she would be in touch with him. When she did so she would bring him the early chapters of her employer's novel.

With this hope, held against all rational argument, Len Stockley reached his office just after nine on the morning after the dance. He had indulged in a miserable breakfast of cornflakes and pale, tasteless coffee at the railway station. After this, following a sleepless night, he was not in good shape to meet the full blast of commercial struggle. A depressed staff, angry creditors, including George Carr, threatening legal action over the delayed payment of royalties to two of his clients, and to cap it all, his principal backer, sorrowful rather than angry.

"He tried to get you yesterday afternoon," his secretary told him after the call.

"You said I was away on business, I hope," Len told her.

"You had not told me that. I did say I thought it was in connection with business, because you were meeting Mr. Trotter."

"How the devil did you know I was meeting Chris?"

She flushed, pursing her mouth.

"You phoned him, using his name. You told him not to meet you at the station."

"Do you always listen to my private calls?"

No answer.

"Well O.K. I shall be out for lunch. I may be back late. If this is all the letters, I've read them and I'll give you the answers now and I'll sign them before I leave."

"Yes, Mr. Stockley."

She usually called him Len, as most people did these days. But he had offended her. O.K. why not? Bloody nosey bitch! Lunch. Well, it was worth lunch to hear Ned's moaning; he was starving and lunch at the backer's club was well worth having. But with nothing to report? What about Judy's old writer? *What* about her?

Len arrived at his own home in Hampstead rather later than usual that evening to find his wife, Clare, stretched out

48

on a long chair in their tiny garden sipping whisky to the accompaniment of her transistor radio, playing pop music at full blast. She turned a lazy head to him but did not speak. He leaned over her to peck her cheek and turn off the noise.

"Sorry I'm late," he said without any noticeable regret in his voice. "Had lunch with Ned and that made me late back in the office to finish the day's work."

"You didn't go back to the office this afternoon," Clare said slowly, in a hard voice. "Because I rang twice and your secretary said you had signed your letters this morning and she did not think you would be in again today."

"She talks too damned freely," Len said, but without much warmth.

"Anyway, if you've had lunch with Ned you won't mind a cold supper, I hope," Clare went on, but made no move to go indoors.

"As long as I get it fairly soon," her husband told her.

He was determined not to quarrel with his wife that night. He was still riding high on his success with Ned, who had swallowed wholesale his brilliant proposition about the book by an unknown author that he had discovered in a twenty-four hour visit to Devon.

Ned had been interested. More than interested, to the tune of added support, Len told Clare, as they ate their limp salad and chopped ham roll at the garden table in the dying sunlight.

"Poor sap," was Clare's only comment.

Though Len agreed inwardly with this verdict, he only gave his wife a sad look and shake of the head as he took his empty plate away indoors. On his way back he stripped a banana he had picked off the fruit dish in the dining annexe of the sitting room, but instead of going back into the garden took it away to the small room he called his study. Chris must be told that the plan he had suggested to Len was definitely on, but it all depended on Judy.

He failed to get Chris on the phone, but he need not have worried. Judy had understood perfectly well what was required of her and had every intention of securing her trip to London.

In the garden Clare waited for Len to come back. It was always the same. From the very start of their marriage he had always refused to have things out with her. She didn't want to quarrel with him; just explain where he was wrong and why, so that he need not make the same old mistake over and over again.

But he never *would* listen and he always took the wrong line, *always*. A pity really, that old friend of his father's, Ned, he called him, though he expected her to give the stupid old fellow his full name, or anyway 'Sir Edgar.'—Ned, the benefactor, an evil influence rather than a good angel. But nothing would ever make him see that. The money the old boy wielded held Len spell bound. The knighthood was for public services. The money came from continuing success in Export and Import Consultancy; what that really was she thought it better not to inquire.

The sky, where soft clouds slowly gathering had quenched the setting sun, brought Clare back from her musing. Her awareness of growing darkness was pointed by the sudden light that came on in Len's study, the window of which faced the garden. She gathered up the meagre remains of their meal and carried the tray into the house.

A bleak evening lay before her. Why did Len never take her out these days? Expense? Perhaps. But just for a walk on the Heath, a chat, like in the old days. Even to go to the pictures? Well, they had the tele, he'd say. What's wrong with the tele? Poor? Old films and old plays? All right, wild life, whodunits, talks. Surely something to look at.

The argument, so familiar, would go back and forth and she could never say to him, "Look, I'm bored! I want to talk to you. I want you to want to talk to me. You're getting further off every day. I'm miserable, Len!"

No good to say any of that to him. She had tried and he only told her not to nag him and went away into that poky little so-called study, all those books he expected her to dust and that heavy desk and his extension of the telephone.

Closing the kitchen door behind her Clare heard the telephone ring, immediately stopped as Len snatched up the receiver. In a quick dash, making no sound with her sandalled feet, she ran across the hall through the open door of the sitting room and with practised care took up the main telephone receiver.

Her worst suspicions were confirmed. A girl's voice, in an accent Clare could not place, was saying, "Yes, I'll come. I've got what you want."

"I'm sure you have. Meet me about five to one at the Little Ox restaurant."

Clare listened, shaking with rage as her husband gave detailed instructions of how the stranger could find her way to the eating house. Len finished his instructions by saying, "Why not take a taxi from the station. I'll add it to the expenses of your trip."

"No need for that," Judy answered gaily. "I'm not exactly on the bread line. Be seeing you."

She must have rung off herself, Clare decided, for Len put down the receiver after saying, "Bye" in a voice charged with feeling. This left Clare with the other receiver in her hand, too numb with fury and grief to realise what she was doing. So that when Len picked up the extension to try again to contact Chris, he got no dialling tone and understood at once what this meant.

Clare dropped the receiver when Len burst into the hall. He shouted, "How dare you! How dare you spy on me!" and rushed towards her with both hands raised.

He could not have used a more misleading accusation. It fed her ready jealousy; she got to her feet to meet him; she was not afraid, had never been afraid of this in-

51

effectual man. His words sustained her to the point of triumph.

"So now we know why you were away overnight. Devon indeed! And late home, too. And making a new date —for—"

Her growing contempt, born of jealous rage, choked her. They stood glaring at one another, Len sickened and ashamed for having lost his head over a non-existent complication.

"You're mad," he said, turning away. "That was a business call. I told you I was in Devon on business. That call confirmed it. A hopeful move."

She laughed bitterly.

"Come off it, you fool! You bloody liar! You unspeakably bungling idiot! Business my aunt fanny! That girl's voice is enough for me. *She* never meant any sort of business except one. Deny that if you can. Got what you want. Of course she has."

"You disgust me," Len told her. He was back in his citadel, about to lower the gates of silence, of withdrawal. It was impossible at this stage to explain about Judy. The whole situation was too delicate. If the plan could go forward, if his half-lies to Ned were justified, then with success he might tell Clare how it all came about. But not now. Far too dangerous.

Clare saw what she had done and did not care. Her jealous exasperation still ruled her.

"You needn't think you'll get away with it!" she cried. "I know the meeting place and the time. Business? O.K. She can meet the boss's wife. That ought to open her eyes a bit."

Len made no answer to this. He stared at her coldly for a few seconds, then turned away and left her. She saw him open and shut the front door as he went quickly away from her. It was only then that she realised she did not know the date of this meeting with the new girl. Her threat was empty. She looked on the desk in his study. There was no note of a date on the telephone pad, only the name 'Little Ox' which she had heard him give. She broke down then and wept tears of defeat.

Meanwhile Len went to a call box down the road and managed to find Chris. He did not explain what had happened, merely told him that Judy had been in touch and that he wanted to change the place of meeting to 'Paul's parlour' instead of 'Little Ox'. Would Chris let her know. He himself did not know her phone number, if she had one.

"She has, but her mum doesn't like her using it," Chris answered, laughing. "O.K. I'll tell her."

Chris frowned as he hung up. The sucker was getting into another of his muddles, was he? Well, no good getting steamed up over him at this stage. Must rely on Judy now. With caution, as always.

VI

"You don't look at all well," George Carr said, severely. "You're working too hard."

"Don't I know it," Anita told him, "It's your fault. Well, not yours alone. Ian's just as bad, always writing to ask for more chapters. Expect me to turn the thing out like a sausage machine."

George laughed.

"The result is totally unlike sausage meat," he assured her. "The freshest of minced beef if you want to continue the metaphor. But seriously, Anita, we don't mean to press you. It's just that the work is developing so splendidly. It's the best thing you've ever done. Astonishing."

He checked his encomium, too late. She was unbearably acute.

"At my age, you mean. Perhaps. Sometimes I'm pleased. More often I'm disgusted with myself for having dried up so long I dare not set a story in modern times, but must go back to my own childhood days."

"*The Eve of Yesterday*," George quoted, looking at the title on the manuscript before him. "Excellent. You always did have a flair for titles."

The buzzer went on his desk. Kate, his secretary, said, "Mr. Macalister is at reception. He says he is in his own car and daren't wait more than five minutes."

"He's taking you for lunch, Anita," George said, rising.

"I'll see you down. Tell him I'll pass this new set of chapters on to him tomorrow. I imagine you're near the end?"

"Fairly near. If I ever get there."

"Don't hurry it. And take a holiday. Working holiday, if you like. Change of scene, anyway."

"What about the typing?"

"Damn the typing! Leave it till you get back or find someone wherever you go. You don't really depend on this girl, do you? She makes a fair number of silly mistakes."

"She's very encouraging, very insistent. And quick."

"Rushes you, does she?"

"A bit. Yes, a good deal. We'd better hurry down, hadn't we? Ian doesn't like waiting. These double yellow lines!"

They found Ian Macalister arguing with a traffic warden over the amount of time allowed for picking up and setting down. Anita, thoroughly flustered by this detestable example of London rush and bustle, sank into the dark blue leather passenger seat of her publisher's large car, forgetting to say goodbye or even wave to George as she glided away.

He went back to his office, vaguely troubled. Anita did look fagged out, not perhaps dangerously so, but after all the old girl was in her seventies and they had all been cheering her on, encouraging, pushing.—He thought suddenly of the Sports Day at his own prep school, so long ago now, and of the Father's Race. Dad had to run to where his son was waiting, then take the little blighter up pick-a-back and run on again to the tape. He remembered his own old father, Frederick, founder and head of the firm he himself now controlled. Dangerous race really. The boys grew heavier as the fathers grew older. Some at thirteen-plus were great louts as tall, even taller, than their sires.

They must consider Anita more. Certainly her new book was quite unexpectedly good and even exciting. But again, how much of that lay in the unusual way it was coming in to him. Not as a finished work but in irregular serial parts. And going on to Haseldyne like that too. They really

55

mustn't push the old lady. He'd have a word with Ian later that day.

Anita herself fully understood the concern her agent and her publisher were showing. Surely it was most unusual for Ian to drive round in his own posh car to pick her up, with George at her elbow to see she did not trip at the pavement edge. They must chat in a business manner on the phone quite frequently, but actual meetings, the heads of two distinguished firms, informally, casually, simply expressing their care for the physical safety of a client, an author they considered too frail to look after herself? Most unusual, surely? Flattering, of course, but alarming, too, not a little.

"It's not as if I was a best-seller, known to be on her last legs," Mrs. Grosshouse told the Hastons in Salcombe, two days after her return to Siddicombe.

They too had shown concern over her repeated expeditions to London. They had invited her to dinner and the evening being fine and warm had suggested that Mervyn would go across on the ferry to fetch her.

"I'll drive myself round," Anita told them. "Do the car good to exercise the poor thing. I haven't had it out all week except to go to the station and back."

And drive she did, though the evening rush hour was not over, and tourist traffic on the narrow Devon roads still building up as the summer advanced.

She arrived hot, dishevelled, her short, straight white hair blown about by the cross wind through the open windows of the car, with a fixed look of exasperation at the many halts, jams and sudden evasions of collision she had endured on the way.

"You look exhausted," Sarah told her reprovingly. "You should have taken Mervyn's offer."

"I hate the ferry," she answered, but quietly, because subdued by the weakness she felt in her legs and the thumping of her heart.

They installed her on a long chair in the winding ample

56

garden, with its rainbow mass of flowers and its superb view over the estuary. They were in the shade now on the eastern side of the hill but the sun still lit up the opposite shore and the rocks and sands away to Prawle Point.

The Hastons supplied her with a generous whisky while Mervyn gave her various items of local news and gossip. Then Sarah came out to take them in to the meal. After it they went out again into the growing dusk for their coffee. Anita refused brandy on account of driving herself home.

"I'm driving," Mervyn told her. "No argument. I'll walk back and use the ferry. Do me good and it's still running till late."

"Please let him," Sarah urged. "Get him in training."

"What for?" The offer was too tempting, but must be argued about before acceptance.

"Italy. We're off at the end of the month." Mervyn looked at his wife. "Tell her what we've got her here for tonight, Sal."

Mrs. Grosshouse sat up. She did not know whether to be amused or angry. They were dears. They were the only real friends she had made in Salcombe. The only civilised ones.

"A conspiracy!" she declared, throwing out her hand so clumsily that she upset her coffee cup. When the mess was cleared and she had exhausted apology, she simply said, "Tell me," and leaned back in her chair again to listen.

Sarah told her that they thought she was looking ill, strained and exhausted. She must be driving herself far too hard. She badly needed a holiday.

"Can't afford it," Mrs. Grosshouse interrupted.

"We know," Sarah answered. "You mustn't mind us knowing, Anita dear. After all you did tell us at the start that you were writing this novel to make money."

"It isn't published yet."

"But it definitely will be?"

"Oh yes. Haseldyne, my old publishers, are quite keen."

"How far have you got?"

"Three-quarters. Roughly. About six chapters left to do, but the length varies. I never quite know what my characters will take it into their heads to do before the thing sets into its appointed end."

"You do appoint the end, then?" Mervyn asked.

"Oh yes. From the beginning. Really from before the beginning."

Sarah broke into this side-tracking with a sharp rebuke.

"Don't lead her off into a literary argument, Vin." She turned again to Mrs. Grosshouse. "You do agree that you need a holiday, Anita?"

"I need to finish my book."

"But could you do that on holiday?"

She stared, not bothering to refute this nonsense.

"Look. We want you to come away with us. To Italy. The North; lakes, mountains. No sight-seeing, unless you want that on your own."

Mrs. Grosshouse still stared, but her inner excitement showed in an altogether fresh sparkle in her faded eyes.

"You see, we've been offered the loan of a villa for up to four months, rent absurdly small, all mod. con. together with domestic help, which is a permanent fixture. It's too big for just us. Vin's got an old buddy of his joining and I'd be so pleased, so honoured, if you'd come too, Anita."

"I can't afford the travel, even if the food and drink would not be more than at home," Mrs. Grosshouse answered. "Besides, there's the typing. I couldn't bring Judy, could I?"

"No," Sarah agreed. She did not think much of Judith Smith, had not expected her to be up to the job. Nothing would induce her to offer a place in the villa to that fancy piece.

"I can type," she said. "I didn't offer when you were looking for someone because—well, because of Vin and the Twilight Homes committee. But—"

Mrs. Grosshouse smiled.

"With domestic service laid on you'll be bored, you mean."

"No, I don't, you darned old cynic!" She laughed, but catching Mervyn's eye went on seriously, "Now, you're not to be offended, but we'd love to put up the travel fares. Vin's friend is in Italy already. No need to bother about him. Just tell him when to expect him at the villa. You'd pay us back the fares when you get the royalty advance. Now, what about it?"

There was further argument and no progress. Mrs. Grosshouse would think it over, she told them. Mervyn drove her home in her own car and succeeded in getting a lift back to Salcombe in a minibus with a load of youngsters who had enjoyed a series of light-hearted lectures the professor had given for the W.E.A. that spring.

Mrs. Grosshouse watched him accept their cheerful hospitality with admiration and a grudging envy. He did not mind their total lack of awe or even respect for his age and standing. He seemed quite to enjoy it. For her own part she was thankful to see a few young people who were neither thugs nor hooligans.

She thought of Judy as she shut her front door behind her, after waving goodbye to the minibus. Could she possibly manage without the girl's help if she brought herself to accept this very tempting offer from the Hastons? No good, really. Even if they lent her the fare she would have so little spending money to take with her it would be embarrassing. What would happen to her pension if she went abroad? No, it was a lovely, enticing dream. She would tell them tomorrow that it was impossible.

But the next day reversed this reluctant decision, for the post brought a letter from George's foreign rights department telling her they had made a sale in West Germany for a new pocket edition of her early novel, *Too Late for the Dawn Chorus*. The contract would follow shortly. The royalties—

"The royalties will make it possible to go with you, Sarah," Anita explained. "Only they won't arrive for several weeks, of course. They never did in the old days, so they probably take even longer now. But if you could lend me—"

"Of course we will. I'll tell Vin to get the tickets right away. We ought to be ready to push off in about three weeks' time."

Three weeks. She could finish the chapter she was on and write one more. No need to declare her plans until nearer the time. Of course not. She did not yet know the exact date.

So it was not until four days before she left that Mrs. Grosshouse spoke to Mrs. Droge in the morning and to Judy that afternoon. It came as a shock to both.

The daily housekeeper was not really surprised. Her old lady had been getting very peculiar of late, working away at this story she said she was writing. No wonder she had worn herself out and the Hastons, retired Oxford don she'd been told, saw she was breaking up and were giving her a nice long holiday.

All this she explained to Judy when the girl, much more upset, went to Mrs. Droge in the kitchen before she left that evening.

"Fired without notice!" she began. "Not that it was ever an official engagement. But without notice of any kind! I ought to complain, oughtn't I?"

"I wouldn't know," Mrs. Droge told her, stiffly. "What about your grant? Should you be taking wages for what you do?"

"I'm obliging her," Judy answered. "What she gives me is nobody's business."

"It certainly isn't mine," Mrs. Droge was nettled. "So you needn't come asking my advice, Miss Smith. Mrs. Grosshouse may be round the bend but she's entitled to spend her time and her money as she likes, I suppose. It's obvious you do that too."

Mrs. Droge turned her back on the girl to occupy herself at the sink. Judy, excellent in direct battle with her contemporaries, was defeated by this show of total indifference and went away. But she was very seriously disturbed.

Next day Mrs. Grosshouse took a small suitcase to deposit at her bank. It held the whole of the longhand manuscript to date of her new novel, together with one carbon of the typed copy made by Judy. She had been surprised to find the carbons made by herself of the first seven chapters before Judy came to help her lying below the subsequent carbons in a mixed-up order, not in sequence. This disturbed her a little but she put it down to the natural confusion she had noticed in the girl's actions of late. From time to time only. Nothing serious. Perhaps her own doing; old age, of course. No girlish inattention; not thinking about the boy-friend, that brash young man, who had come to pick her up one evening. Please God she could finish this book. Thank God for the Hastons and their borrowed villa in Italy.

Judy wasted no time in telling Chris Trotter about the abrupt end of her job and the author's departure abroad.

"Where to?"

"I don't know. She didn't say the country. Or who with. Just gave me my money as usual and thanked me for what I'd done."

"No date for coming back?"

"No. Does it matter?"

"Of course it matters, you nit. Will she finish her book after she comes back? Will she have you to type it?"

"She didn't say. I told you, didn't I? Is it my fault the old bitch is off her nut?"

She had been screaming at him and was out of breath. After a pause she said, more quietly, "If you want to know, I don't think that blessed novel will ever be finished. I think she's dropped it."

61

Chris stiffened. That was impossible. It couldn't happen. Not to him. Not to Len. Good grief, not to Len!

"You realise," he said slowly, in the low, menacing voice she detested, "it will ruin Len if he can't publish this book. It will ruin the old biddy, too. And no more trips to London for you, my girl."

She would mind that, he knew. Perhaps not enough yet for one solution his fertile mind was already considering. So what else.

"We'll have to have her address," he said. "You see that, don't you? Don't you darling?" he repeated, drawing her close. "You'll get her address for me, won't you?"

Judy pulled away. Endearments from Chris meant nothing. The cold contempt in his eyes, seen at close quarters as he kissed her, did not deceive her for a moment. But there was sense in what he said. If they had to find out whether Mrs. Grosshouse was finishing her novel or not they must find out where she was. There was just one person who could tell her and that was Kate Ford, the daughter of the minister, vicar they called him, at Siddicombe. But she wouldn't explain that to Chris.

"I'll try," she said.

"Of course you'll try. Who was it got you that job? Bint in your own class, wasn't it? Old-fashioned name. Mabel. Hester. Kate. It was Kate, wasn't it?"

So he knew. He always knew. Judy accepted defeat. She promised to get the address.

Feeling partly restored, Chris drove over to Uncle and Aunt Frobisher on Friday evening, accepting the inevitable invitation to stay for the weekend. During it he made two telephone calls to Len Stockley.

On the following Monday evening Chris was able to pass to Judy the publisher's urgent request to meet him at his office on Thursday next at noon.

VII

Kate Ford, always willing to be helpful, consulted her mother over the whereabouts of the Hastons.

Mrs. Ford was surprised.

"Didn't you know? They're in Italy and they've taken Mrs. Grosshouse with them."

"I know. That's why I'm asking. I mean Judy Smith, you know, the girl who's been helping Mrs. Grosshouse—well, the old dame's fired her and not even told her why."

Mrs. Ford considered. Yes, she knew Judy Smith. It was hard luck she'd lost the job, but it wasn't her business to know where her employer had gone or with whom, was it?

"No, I suppose not," Kate agreed.

Mrs. Ford relented.

"It was Italy," she said, "but that's all I know. I should think the housekeeper, Mrs. Droge, will have the address, so as to forward letters."

"Good idea," Kate said, pleased to have an answer ready. She did not know Judy well, though she admired her looks, or said she admired them, as did everyone else. She would not care to disappoint Judy. Everyone at college knew you would be unwise to do so. There was something strong, deep down, something very persistent, very determined, about Judy. She never gave up when she wanted something.

"About that address where Mrs. Grosshouse has gone,"

she said the next time she saw Judy. "Mother says it's in Italy and Mrs. Droge will have it to forward letters. Or else her bank. She goes to ours, I know."

She named the bank and the branch and Judy appeared to be satisfied.

Chris was not. Unlooked-for expense and he wouldn't be able to take Judy to Italy. Far too pricey. But they had to know if the old cow was going on with her writing, or if she'd given up, written herself out, as a lot of young hopefuls did and *they* hadn't one foot in the grave, like Mrs. Grosshouse. Besides, without the address in Italy it was no good thinking of going there. He wouldn't be able to interview her, even if he could give out he was representing a literary agent; far too risky. He had to keep right in the background all the way. Judy must get the address from Mrs. Droge.

This was easier said than done. The girl found the cottage totally deserted, locked up, curtains drawn on the ground floor. At the Post Office shop in Siddicombe she learned that Mrs. Droge was also away; she had gone to spend a month with her sister in London. No, she couldn't give the address, but letters would be forwarded.

"I didn't actually want to write to Mrs. Droge herself," Judy said, in desperation. "I wanted her to give me Mrs. Grosshouse's address in Italy. I was helping the old lady with some typing. I just wanted to ask her something."

"We are forwarding Mrs. Grosshouse's letters, too," Phyllis Good, the post-mistress, told her. "If you write to her at her home address we will send it on, provided you use the correct postage and put Please Forward on it."

"What a rigmarole!" Judy exclaimed crossly.

Mrs. Good gave a short laugh.

"More of a safeguard," she said. "Can I do anything else for you, dear?"

"I'll have an airmail letter for Europe."

Judy tried to smile, tried to suggest the whole matter was unimportant. She did not deceive the post-mistress.

Chris was furious, more than ever determined to find that address. If Siddicombe wouldn't disgorge, he'd have to winkle it out himself. It was bound to be in the cottage somewhere. He had never forgotten the skills he had learned and practised in his adolescence, while managing to avoid trouble by passing it, as a rule, to others.

Siddicombe, in the meantime, stimulated by Mrs. Ford's suspicions of Judy Smith, had expanded the girl's quite simple attempt to get her former employer's address into a plot to rob the old woman's cottage.

The rumour reached the police in Feltbridge, who warned their patrol, accustomed to tour Siddicombe and the neighbouring villages once a week, to pay particular attention to Mrs. Grosshouse's cottage on his next round.

It produced results, for the constable discovered some fragments of white paint below the kitchen window at the back of the small house. This suggested a possible breaking and entering and on following it up a detective sergeant from the Feltbridge police station was able to get the cottage keys from the post-mistress to whom Mrs. Droge had entrusted them. Mrs. Grosshouse had authorised Mrs. Droge to pass the keys to Phyllis Good if she left Siddicombe for more than twenty-four hours, the detective sergeant learned.

Naturally Chris knew nothing of these arrangements, but he need not have worried in any case. He had found nothing that he wanted, so he had taken nothing, broken nothing. For nothing was locked up, since Mrs. Grosshouse had taken all the longhand and carbon scripts of her book to the bank and in addition her few pieces of valuable china, silver and jewellery. So Chris was not tempted to turn from his main purpose to simple pilfering.

But the very fact that the police visits were almost completely unproductive led the Force to take more trouble over the case than they might otherwise have done. Not only did they notify Mrs. Grosshouse of their limited discovery, a single palm-print on the kitchen window sill, unidentified in the local or Plymouth records, but they would like to hear from Mrs. Grosshouse if there was any property of hidden or unusual value present in the cottage when she left for Italy, so that they could check that it had not been taken or damaged.

As for the village rumours, relayed to them by the Siddicombe post-mistress, the police decided that, as usual, they were nonsense. The girl, Judy Smith, had wanted Mrs. Grosshouse's address. She had been told she could write to the cottage and the letter would be forwarded. She had bought an airmail letter and done exactly that. Her letter had been forwarded. The girl's father, contacted casually at his usual pub one evening, had explained that his daughter was staying away with a friend. She had certainly not been in Devon for the last two weeks. The college term was over. Mid-July. Like the schools.

Anyway, the palm-print was too big for a girl, unless she was a very big girl and they did come giant size sometimes these days. But Judy was only average and smashing to look at, by all accounts. So what about her friends? Well, what about them? Practically no girls, but legions of boys. The local Force gave up, but left the incident on the files.

Mrs. Grosshouse was surprised to have a letter from Judy, forwarded by Phyllis Good. She was always surprised by kindness and consideration and she could see no other motive behind this example of it. She meant to write back to thank the girl, but the final chapters of her novel were going ahead and absorbing all her energy in a quick final burst of production. So she never did answer Judy's offering and Judy's hope of discovering her address, or at least the name of the town in Italy on a picture postcard, was unfulfilled.

"I never thought she would answer," Chris told her.

He had come up to London again for the weekend, the third weekend running.

"I ought to go home," Judy said. "It's hopeless, isn't it? The old bag's given it up, this novel, I mean. Len says so. He ought to know. He might have taken it, to publish, I mean. But if she isn't ever going to finish it the whole thing's off. Right?"

"No. At least, wouldn't it be a shame after all the work you've done on it, you and Len?"

She frowned.

"I ought to go home," she repeated. "They don't know where I am. I said with Sylvia. Dad wouldn't know—always so bloody vague, except when he goes fishing. But Mum might begin to wonder. *She* wouldn't really mind what happened to me, but she does mind the neighbours. Anyway, you don't really own this flat, do you, Chris? When are they supposed to be coming back?"

He was suddenly furious. So dumb and then suddenly she'd rumble something he'd thought not possible.

"Mind your effing business!" he roared at her.

Because that was exactly what she *was* doing and was determined to continue doing, she made no answer, simply stared at him, her beauty frozen into an icy mask, silent but menacing. If Chris had not been so intent upon his own frustrations he might have understood the reversal in their positions. He was no longer the leader.

Judy went home to Plymouth after the weekend. She had one more session with Len on Sunday, at which she had to acknowledge that she had not been able to get in touch with Mrs. Grosshouse. She did not know the address in Italy, nor did Chris. It would look funny if she went on trying to find out any more about the Hastons or her former employer, who was with them. So perhaps they had better give up the whole idea of helping Mrs. Grosshouse by publishing her book.

"She must have given up," Judy decided sadly.

Len understood her perfectly. For the last three weeks, under his supervision and with his constant help, they had edited and revised the whole of the novel, using those carbon copies Judy had made and brought to London. Together they had, he hoped, altered it beyond any superficial skimming by critics. He had taken it to Ned for approval and earned for it a surprised enthusiasm.

"But it's magnificent," his elderly backer had exclaimed. "Why don't you put it in for a prize? It isn't a first novel, is it? I thought you told me the author is an old woman."

"No," he had answered. "Quite young and her first book."

Ned's face changed. This was a lie and he knew the truth. Or rather, what Chris had told him as the truth, which was that the old woman's book no longer existed to threaten them for too much editing. She would keep quiet for money, her prime object in trying to write. Chris's jacket was already drawn and in production. The prepared copies were marked. But to take over the authorship? Highly risky, unless they worked fast.

When Judy heard a slightly amended account of Len's interview with his backer and the latter's praise of the book, she stared at him, astonished. Not by his confession of blatant lying, though she did not even now know the full extent of it, but that he had told her of it. Of course the book had been Chris's idea from the start. It was just like him. He was to have the job of drawing the jacket and that meant money and promotion, she supposed in establishing himself as a commercial artist. But was it really like Len? Well, the poor bugger did seem to be on the skids in his business and he wasn't a strong character like Chris—or like what Chris thought of himself.

But Len was looking at her, pleadingly, pathetically. She said, in a voice that showed no surprise whatever, "You actually told him the book is by me? And he thinks you ought to put it in for a prize of some sort? Ya, I know they have these so-called book prizes. But it isn't finished is it? So won't ever be published, we think. Don't we? Or are *you* going to finish it?"

"With your help, of course."

She became very wary. This was unexplored territory as far as she was concerned, and therefore highly dangerous. She had heard at the college of that thing called plagy— something. Mostly snitching ideas from films, tele plays or features. They milked you dry and then produced something they called their own or said it was coincidence. But a whole book? Besides, Len could fix it so she'd have to carry the can if anything went wrong.

"I'm not a writer," she protested. "You'd be responsible."

"I'd publish it," Len assured her and explained some of the detail of the operation. "You would have a contract with my firm, the usual form of contract. I'll explain that. You can use a pseudonym, a pen name."

"What's that?"

"A name you write under that is not your own name."

"So nobody'd know it was me."

"That's the idea. You could keep Judith as the first name. Just think up a new surname. Ned thinks the book might do for entering for one of the autumn prizes if the end matches the beginning."

"With you writing the end."

"And you—er—polishing the dialogue to bring it up to date."

"I thought it was supposed to be period? Edwardian?"

"The public likes costume, but familiar dialogue."

Judy laughed. A full, raucous laugh, head thrown back, lovely mouth wide open.

It was the first time Len had heard Judy laugh and it startled him. It was revealing. It showed him that though she was poorly endowed with intellect and lamentably under educated, in natural low cunning, directed to base

69

ends, she might prove to be unusually gifted, which included an uncomfortable sense of humour.

He smiled back, a weak shamefaced smile. But his eyes were bright, which Judy found reassuring. She did not notice the small pupils. But she would not have known their significance if she had done so. Why should she? It seemed she must either drop this thing altogether or trust Len to see it through. If it blew up in their faces, as she thought it very well might, there would be lies each of them could bring forward and she decided hers would go down better than his. Apart from Chris.

"Does Chris know what you want me to do?" she asked.

"Of course. He will design the jacket. It was his idea at first to get me to publish for this Mrs. Grosshouse. Make a splash for a first novel for an old woman. Win a big commission from her for himself, and do me a bit of good, too. In return for help I've given him from time to time. And on condition he designed this jacket himself and used Ned's firm for making up, binding and all that."

"Help," Judy asked slowly. "Help you've given Chris, or blackmail?"

She had said it on the spur of the moment, not really intending it seriously. The effect on Len was marked. He did not change colour but he stiffened. For the first time Judy felt genuine unease; not physical fear; this middle-aged town-bred man was too soft, too unfit, too unused to real muscular effort of any kind to hold a menace for her. She was quite capable of taking him on and winning too in any natural trial of physical strength. She had not defeated the many attempts of her west country boy-friends, to fall a victim to this publisher's anger. But the extreme seriousness of his reaction was enlightening. Chris had levied help from Len, or was it Len and Ned, the unseen backer. Len and Ned. Or really Ned? Blackmail for Chris, from Ned through Len. *How? Why?*

When the silence between them became unbearable

Judy said, as flippantly as she could manage with the iron barrier of his wrath between them, "Oh, it was Chris all along, was it? I always thought he might be some sort of a louse. He's been teasing your backer, this Ned you haven't let me meet, has he?"

Len groaned aloud. It was obscene that a girl with the face of an innocent angel should be so familiar with every form of wickedness, should wade through the mucky sewers of life in a state of blank indifference, untouched by it. He groaned because he knew that was impossible. Not untouched, which was impossible, but indifferent because she was as incapable of moral understanding as—

His own hypocrisy rose and hit him in the face. No point beefing over moral issues. He had given them up long ago and never as solidly and fatally as now. Both Ned and he were up to their necks in a business practically on the rocks. Two businesses, the older one the more dangerous. Chris Trotter was only the catalyst that had started the final rot with his wicked demands. And even wickeder suggestions. As luck or fate had ordered, the old woman's unfinished book might well provide their escape—through more wickedness—to freedom, perhaps security.

"It's really up to us now," Len said, in a new harsh voice. "You and me, Judy. We can forget Chris. He's done his job introducing you and the manuscript to my firm. Now we've got to push it through—the project, I mean. This book. I'll finish it and you must come up a few more times to edit it the way you have been doing, which is just right. Or stay in town, preferably, to be on hand when I'm ready for you. But go home for a bit now. Damp down any nonsense gossip there."

"I'm not going near Siddicombe again. Catch me!" Judy told him.

"Well, perhaps not. Let that slide on to Chris if you can. Of course you can."

He smiled at her again and she smiled back. The next

71

morning she went home to Plymouth. There were no letters for her; no picture postcard from Italy. The old bitch can take what's coming to her, Judy decided. Only don't let any of it slide on to me.

VIII

The Young Adventurers by Julia Trebannon, was published in September. It was set in early Edwardian times and dealt with the trials and loves of several young people in their struggles against the social constraints, resultant revolts, failures, tragedies and ultimate success of the young hero and heroine. Not at all an original theme, the critics said at once, taking a gratifying interest in the book, but deeply romantic and most uncommonly well researched for a first novel by a reputedly young author.

The judges in the 'Golden Sunrise' First Novel Prize thought the same. In October they finished working through a depressing pile of intimate tales of psychological stress, insanity, fantasy and violence, where the characters, mostly urban, struggled to their deaths with very little movement, except in bed, and no apparent material support of any kind, social security being taken for granted, so not mentioned.

The news of his and Judy's success came to Len as a dauntingly welcome surprise. He could not at first believe it. The book had got off to a fairly good start, since it had pleased the more distinguished critics. To have brought off, by way of the prize, best-selling status, was overwhelming. And distinctly frightening.

He rang up Ned at once. The latter had agreed with the critics, anticipated getting his money back in more ways than one and took the news calmly.

"Have you told the girl?"

"Not yet."

"Or Chris?"

"No. Should I? Or wait till the actual prize giving ceremony is lined up? Where do they have it?"

"It's run by an oil consortium, isn't it? The one that has a few other irons in the fire as well."

Len felt a small twinge of distaste which he suppressed.

"Yes. That's right. I think they use one of the best-known hotels for the occasion. I shall be notified of the details in due course. Do I tell Judy at once, then, or Chris?"

After a pause Ned said slowly, "Come along here this evening, Len. About six. Right?"

Judy heard the news that night at her home in Plymouth. It was given her by Ned, in very guarded terms. The first novel by the young author Julia Trebannon was doing very nicely, very nicely indeed. There would be news of it in the papers the next day, probably. So she would be wise not to say anything at all about her part in its production. Not in Plymouth; not at the college, certainly not at Siddicombe or to anyone connected with the village. She understood, didn't she?

"Of course I understand," Judy answered. Even Ned, the purse-strings, chose to think she was thick, which was a hell of a boob, as he'd better understand in future.

She waited for an answer to her sharply spoken rejoinder but none came. So she went on, "Don't you think I'd better come up to town again? Chris is still there, I think. He's not here. He might be at his uncle's at Minehead. What does *he* think about this?"

She was interrupted by her mother's voice, shrill, complaining.

"Your supper's getting cold. Stop nattering with whoever it is."

She covered the mouthpiece of the receiver long enough

to shout back, "Nearly finished," and then said softly to Ned, "Mum's creating. Where do I go if I come up? Chris, I suppose? Same place?"

"No." Ned was positive. "I'll arrange with Len and get him to ring you tomorrow. Yes, you'll be needed here quite soon. Don't bother Chris. We're looking after him, too."

Judy hung up and joined her mother and father in the dining area of their lounge. She was silent during the meal, partly because she had to eat fast to catch up with her parents, chiefly she needed time to take in just what Ned had been on about. Well, he had good news for her over that book they'd nicked from old Grosshouse. She knew they'd put it in for a prize, so-called Book Prize. Girls she knew well enough to ask at the College had told her newspapers ran them and readers' clubs and literary societies. How much? Depended on the importance or otherwise of the organisers. Well, but on average? As much as a hundred pounds?

"Certainly," one girl said. "You see about them in the papers. There was one written up got the writer a thousand."

"*Pounds*?" Judy asked, suddenly breathless.

"Apparently. You know someone putting in for one?"

"She was going about with that Chris Trotter. He was always on about his publisher friends."

This was a new voice, alien, vaguely unfriendly. Judy had moved away. A thousand pounds. For Ned and Len? For Chris? For herself? Yes, herself. It had to be for herself, Julia Trebannon. Julia—not Judith. She'd made the change herself. Sounded better, slightly foreign—Len had agreed.

"You're very quiet," her mother said, again sharp and complaining. "Who was that on the phone?"

"Sylvia," Judy answered quietly. "You know, where I've been staying in London. Looks like she wants me to help her again."

"What for?" Judy's father asked, suddenly curious.

"Junk shop," she answered. "Really, Dad, I've told you often enough. You never really listen, do you?"

"That's enough," her mother said. "If you've finished, you can help me wash up."

At Ned's house Len heard the phone conversation with Judy on the extension. He listened to the conclusion aghast.

"She can't come up to Chris's flat again," he said. "I mean, where he was. He has to get out not later than tomorrow. He's been worried. The people are to be back in the afternoon."

"He will be out," Ned answered him. "And no, Judy can't join him. I suggest she stays with you and Clare for a few days."

"Oh no!" Len was horrified.

"Why not?"

"Clare doesn't believe me when I insist Judy is merely temporary staff in the office."

Ned was openly contemptuous.

"Did you expect her to? A ridiculous idea! Temporary staff! You must have been out of your mind, knowing how basically jealous Clare always was and always will be!"

"It wasn't easy to explain what she was doing, was it?"

"Why not? A young, very young, writer, bringing you the manuscript of her first novel. Promising effort, needing a fair amount of editing—"

"That's what I said or implied, wasn't it?"

"So vaguely that a person like Clare could not possibly believe it. No, my boy, you deserve all you get from Clare. And I insist you put matters right between you by asking Judy to stay in your house until after the presentation. Just explain to Clare what you are likely to get out of it for yourself. That ought to sweeten the situation in spite of Judy's looks. Incidentally we must keep the Press photographers off her till after the ceremony. You kept the jacket clean, I hope?"

76

"Not even a blown-up family snap and not a single biographical note."

"Good. There could hardly be a reaction from Italy in any case. As far as we know this Mrs. Grosshouse went away with friends, leaving her book unfinished. If she stays away she may never get to know that its double or shadow or whatever else you like to call it has mopped up more, far more, than anything she may have hoped to get. We must try to keep it that way, mustn't we?"

"I suppose so," Len said grudgingly. He found Ned's caution rather chilling, but it was meant to protect them both. Chris was a different matter.

"Have you told Chris yet?" he asked. "You told me to wait."

"I repeat that," his patron ordered. "I think we both know about how far young Chris can be trusted. You will leave it to me to decide when and how to deal with him."

Thankfully, but without verbal agreement, Len did so, and went home to do battle with his wife over taking the girl, Julia Trebannon, prize-winner, into their home during the various public activities connected with her success. Promotion was a word Clare would understand.

She chose to give it a meaning.

"Here!" she cried. "In my house!"

"Our house."

"Entertain your latest mistress in your own house with your wife as hostess? Promotion indeed!"

"Judy is *not* my mistress. I want to promote her book and if staying here helps on her sales that is why I want you to invite her."

"Nothing will ever induce me to invite her," Clare thundered. "Isn't there a boy-friend somewhere in the picture? You used to bring him out in the early days. Before this young bitch came on the scene, actually. I always thought he was one of Ned's boy-friends. Don't tell me his feelings work in both directions. Chris, I mean."

"You have a mind like a sewer," Len muttered, groaning inwardly over his worn cliché, but too miserably sick, all of a sudden, of the whole business, to care what Clare thought or felt.

She saw the sudden change in his mood and was warned by it. He had been very unpredictable for months. She thought she knew enough of his addiction to leave its mild course to Ned's management. But now success was making him reckless. Must she indulge him yet again?

"All right," he suddenly declared. "I'll arrange an hotel room for Judy, which will be expensive and which I shall have to pay for. She will be a prey to the Press as soon as they know where she is, and trust them to find out. They'll be on to her for the childhood story, the parents story, the boy-friend story and I shouldn't wonder if they winkle out the Grosshouse story too, and ruin the whole business—!"

He checked himself abruptly, but too late.

"Grosshouse?" Clare asked slowly. "Just what does that mean?"

So he had to tell her, knowing that Ned would be justly furious if he heard of it. But he did not understand Clare's coldly sensible view of Ned's position in their lives and of Ned's power. She would be discreet unless pushed.

So Clare wrote a letter of prim congratulation to Judy, addressing it, under Len's direction, to Miss Judith Smith, c/o Leonard Stockley, publisher, at the office address. He posted it himself the following day.

Judy enjoyed her stay with Len and Clare. She went to their flat two days before the prize-giving ceremony, a little apprehensive but prepared to behave according to her former school teacher's given rules of upper-class behaviour, as modified to some extent by old Mrs. Grosshouse. This seemed to work quite well. She could see that Clare did not really approve of her and she guessed the cause. She saw too that Len was grateful for her quiet

78

submissive approach and that he admired her for it.

The very small advance publicity that Ned was prepared to allow gratified the Press, particularly as the photographer got a single session with the strikingly beautiful young author, on condition they did not publish until after the prize-giving. With a visual boost of this order in view, the girl's extremely ordinary past and background did not matter at all. She was lined up for a live television interview on the evening after the prize-giving.

The ceremony itself Judy found unexpectedly dull. Far too crowded, with mostly middle-aged and elderly people of both sexes, crowding together in groups, shouting their heads off in posh accents of varying degrees of gentility, staring at her and turning away, or pushing close to demand an introduction, with smiles on their lips and eyes filled with envy or malice.

Len, hovering at her elbow, explained who all these people were. The judges she had met before and these greeted her kindly, but the youngest, the only attractive one among them, was absent; delayed, they told her, but he did not turn up. There were the various presidents or chairmen of various literary clubs and groups of writers, all there to prove their devotion to Letters in whatever form it gained the limited patronage peculiar to the British Isles.

There was too a fair sprinkling of foreign men and women, chiefly European, very knowledgeable in literature past and present. They, in contrast to the photographer, and some of her fellow British, did not treat Judy as a precocious, pretty child, an infant prodigy in one of those odd, regrettable activities, the Arts, but rather as a welcome addition to the tiny band of talent recognised.

And of course the New World attended in considerable strength, again showing Judy uninhibited friendliness. Those in the book business had already lined her up for publication and were gratified to see how the sales would shoot up on the strength of her likeness alone, with film and television to follow almost automatically.

All this, together with a succession of drinks and only a few nuts to eat, put Judy into a stupor that was to blur her memory of the great event so that she never really did justice to recounting it in later times. But of course her powers of description and comment were very limited, her imagination small, her vocabulary poor. At the time her near silence and glazed expression were put down to becoming modesty.

Len became a little anxious about her, for though he had feared she might get over-excited and burst into the sort of foul-mouthed hysterical shouting he had heard sometimes from her contemporaries, he was much more anxious when it seemed possible that she would pass out before she actually received the prize.

However, he did not yet know Judith Smith. Her strong ego was quite capable of enduring any form of trial so long as it held advantage for her. As this strange, boring, raucous, word-beating crowd certainly did. So she stood quite firmly and smiled and listened and said very little. She seemed to drink rather a lot but actually she sipped only a few drops at a time. She was very patient. Ned had explained the terms of her contract to her and she trusted Ned, for his aims were the same as her own. He went much further in ready dishonesty than poor old Len and bitchy jealous Clare, and vain, reckless Chris. She admired Ned. Even now her only contact with him had been on the telephone, but she hoped to meet him in due course. She realised one could not push it.

It did not come to her until the next day that Chris had not been at the prize-giving ceremony. But then she had not seen him more than twice since Mrs. Grosshouse went to Italy with the Hastons. All the time she was working with Len on the last part of her book—yes, *her* book—he had kept away, letting her use the flat sometimes, until he had to get out of it himself. Well, of course he had wanted to run her as a kind of stooge in pulling off his own schemes for getting money from Len and Ned. Obviously he'd fallen down on that. So what? She'd ditch him herself any time now. Fifteen thou at least, Ned told her, what with the prize and the royalties, as they called them. To start with. More if the book went into real best-seller sales. And no need to hide it up at home any longer. As Julia Trebannon she could astonish her West Country circle. Ned said so.

On the third day after the prize-giving, when pictures and press stories of the lovely young writer had given place to the latest brutal rape, a body was taken from the Thames below Teddington.

It was that of a young man, naked, of medium height and build, with naturally curly hair of collar length only, with short sideburns and otherwise a two-day growth of fair hair on his face. The post-mortem showed that he had met his death by drowning and had no outward sign of injury of any kind. The internal examination showed no form of disease, but in due course the stomach and blood contents revealed a large excess of alcohol. He seemed to have been a healthy, well-nourished and well-kept young man, not an addict of any kind. It was judged that the body had been in the water for about five days. Since there were no means of identifying him by his possessions, for he had none with him, careful records were made of his teeth, hair, hand and foot prints. In recording the mouth one fresh observation was made. Some small green algae were found caught between the teeth and these were of a fresh-water species. Further tests of the stomach and lung contents revealed purely fresh water, no salt at all, though the body had been recovered from the tidal part of the river.

These records did not match with anyone on the metropolitan list of missing persons, so his discovery was notified generally and the body was stored away in the refrigerator to await events.

IX

With strong encouragement from the Hastons, Mrs. Grosshouse was persuaded to send her final six chapters of *The Eve of Yesterday*, typed carefully by Sarah without a single blemish, one by one to Ian Macalister of Haseldyne, direct. He welcomed them in six encomiums of growing enthusiasm.

All of which was very comforting for Anita Armstrong, particularly when the advance royalty on the completed manuscript arrived from George Carr, together with the exciting further news that a new English paperback edition of *Too Late for the Dawn Chorus* would be issued very shortly to remind readers in the mature age range that the author of their former favourite was about to match her early triumph with a new superlative work.

"I ought to go home, I think," Mrs. Grosshouse said, beaming with unusual gentleness and gratitude at her friends. "You've been wonderful, both of you. I would never have finished the thing without you. I really can't—"

To their utter surprise and not a little embarrassment Anita Armstrong put her head down on the verandah breakfast table and relapsed into tears.

Clearly it was getting on for time to take the poor old thing back to Devon. Mervyn was alarmed by her emotional breakdown, but Sarah told him it was altogether natural and was good for her. Besides, their temporary lease of the villa had not yet quite run out.

"If she hadn't boxed herself up for the last twenty years she would probably have begun to write again long ago and not waited until she was practically broke," Sarah reminded him. "Hiding herself away at Siddicombe where no one had ever heard of Anita Armstrong, not even the Fords."

"Well, would you expect it?" Mervyn argued. "After all that Dawn book was just a best-seller, among several others of the breed."

"There never are more than two or three at a time."

"Granted. But most of their authors run a few follow-ups, don't they? Enough to establish them permanently as popular writers of the middle-brow library success type, favoured, you would think, by the Fords and their like."

"You forget Anita married her American before her next book after Dawn was published. She was in the U.S. after that and very popular there, just right for those Book Clubs that buy umpteen thousand. Haseldyne published them all here and they did reasonably well, I think. All of them."

Mervyn looked at his wife with amusement.

"I'm not running her down, or the books," he said. "I certainly hope this one will be a success, if only to make her secure in her old age. And of course we do seem to be short of her kind of literate, middle-brow, intelligent story, without violence, nor smeared over with four-letter words. Under-valued and under-praised, on the whole, like the admirable Frank Swinnerton. Judging by what we've seen of it she manages to give a very good idea of manners and morals at the turn of the last century."

"Big of you!" Sarah told him, laughing in her turn.

So the three friends from England set about arranging to go back to Devon, the fourth to his permanent home near Florence. They wound up their four months' occupation of the villa and paid off the temporary staff; an occasion of mixed good nature, goodwill and cupidity on both sides. They secured seats on a mid-week flight where illness had caused vacancies. They notified their various relations and helpers in England of their return.

Mrs. Grosshouse wrote at some length to Mrs. Droge. She had not taken any steps to solve the mystery of the non-burglary at her cottage. She had heard from the post-mistress and from her housekeeper that nothing had been taken as far as they knew and that the police had apparently given up trying to find the culprit.

Siddicombe had now decided that it was the work of one of 'they gipsies'; the police, on the other hand thought it was much more likely to have been one of several juveniles belonging to the village whom they already had in mind, but had not yet been able to prove delinquent.

Mrs. Grosshouse, in her letter, asked Mrs. Droge to air the sheets well, lay the sitting room fire, because she would feel the change to a colder climate and buy in the usual groceries for the coming week.

She also wrote to Ian Macalister and to George Carr to give them the exact date of her return to England, asking at the same time for the expected date of the publication of *The Eve of Yesterday*. She knew that they both had wanted it to catch the autumn reviews when the best critics would be back from their summer holidays. Including the survivors among those older literary pundits, her contemporaries, who might remember her pre-war triumphs as actual happenings, not hearsay or myth.

At the airport she picked up a couple of paperbacks to read on the journey. Both were recent productions, one a crime story by a very well-known name, the other a first novel, a prize-winner, by a young woman called Julia Trebannon. It was called *The Young Adventurers*, a period romance. Mrs. Grosshouse had been led to it by seeing the surname, clearly Cornish. The jacket had a young couple in late Victorian clothes locked closely in a very un-Victorian embrace.

She was called away from the bookstall by the Hastons who had heard their flight number called, so she slipped both books into her bag and hurried off to join her friends. She read the crime story during the journey. She did not touch the other until she went through her hand luggage the next morning in her cottage at Siddicombe.

Even then she threw the period romance on one side, half regretting she had bothered to buy it, except that she had always been interested to discover what productions found favour in the eyes of the modern judges for literary prizes.

But in the middle of the morning she had a telephone call from Haseldyne. Was Miss Armstrong back from Italy? Mr. Macalister wished to speak to her personally. It was very urgent.

"Miss Armstrong speaking," she answered, wondering why the urgency.

"Anita? Ian here. Are you well? Not upset by the journey I hope? You can only just have got back."

"Yesterday evening, as I wrote you in my letter. Ian, what has happened?"

"I must see you right away. I would like to come down to you. I won't inflict another two days travelling on you. Can you get me a room in a nearby hotel? Is there one in Siddicombe?"

"Nothing nearer than Salcombe and that's across the harbour. I could put you up myself if you like. But why the panic? What's it all about?"

"I can't explain on the phone. Forgive me, but it really is important."

Mrs. Grosshouse felt a distinct chill down her spine.

"Not a hitch in the production? The book isn't going to be delayed, is it? No accident—?"

She had become breathless and it showed in the shaky squeak that had transformed her speech. Ian Macalister groaned inwardly. This thing might *kill* her! But how tell her? His nerve failed him and he simply hung up.

For nearly a minute Mrs. Grosshouse sat staring at the quietly buzzing receiver in her hand before she put it back on the rest. Something had happened to *The Eve of Yesterday,* that was obvious. Ian was coming down—unheard of—to explain what that meant. It must be too bad to be borne if it was too difficult to explain by word of mouth. So what, in God's name, could it be?

For an hour Mrs. Grosshouse moved about her cottage, sometimes opening and reading the mail that had arrived since the end of forwarding, sometimes stopping this operation to find Mrs. Droge and ask her about the latter's extended holiday and subsequent activities in the village. The gossip proved that the strange abortive burglary had roused local feeling on her behalf. Her neighbours evidently regarded her as an asset in their society. They knew all about her recent literary activities; they admired her courage at her age in attempting anything longer and more important than a contribution to the parish magazine. Mrs. Ford had tried to explain that the old lady had been a writer in her young days, but no one, including the vicar's wife and daughter, knew what she had written. There was nothing in the name of Grosshouse in the travelling library that came to Siddicombe once a fortnight.

Mrs. Droge was able to report that as far as she knew that Plymouth girl, Judy Smith, had never been seen in Siddicombe since Mrs. Grosshouse left, except on one occasion when she wanted to find out the address in Italy where the Hastons had got a villa.

"Rented," Mrs. Grosshouse told the housekeeper, whose imagination tended to expand all the news she was told. "For four months only. It was lovely, wonderful. I enjoyed every minute of it."

"I'm very glad to hear it," Mrs. Droge said, getting on with her work.

Mrs. Grosshouse wanted to add that she had finished her book there, but in view of Ian's call she refrained.

About an hour later George Carr rang up. Mrs. Grosshouse, recognising his voice got in first with her now seething anxiety.

"George! What on earth's happening? Ian rang up just now. He's coming straight down here. He wouldn't say why. Just rang off. Tell me, George! What's happening?"

"Ian's a bloody fool to scare you without explaining. Something does seem to have happened. A direct plagiarism. Blatant, apparently. But Ian has the complete manuscript, of course."

"Not *The End of Yesterday*?" Mrs. Grosshouse felt sick.

"Apparently. The trouble is it's won one of these commercial prizes."

"*What* has won a prize? *My book!*"

The screech that came to his ears frightened George considerably. He regretted attempts to explain by blower; far better to have written a long letter. But Macalister was raving, invoking the Law before they had the barest facts clear.

"Listen, Anita. Try to cool it. I know it sounds dreadful, But we've got to assess—"

"Don't preach, George. Just tell me. Quickly!"

He did. A very young writer had written a period romance called *The Young Adventurers* about a late Victorian, early Edwardian couple. It had been published by a very new publisher called Leonard Stockley and entered for a literary prize called 'Golden Sunrise', for first novels by young authors. A girl called Julia Trebannon, home in the west country, was the author. It appeared to be almost an exact copy of *The Eve of Yesterday*.

"What did you say the title was?"

"*The Young Adventurers*."

"Then I have it! I bought a paperback at the airport, but I bought two and the other one was more interesting, so I haven't even looked at it again, but I've still got it. I'll go and get it. Hold on!"

"No! Anita, I can't—"

But she had gone, leaving her receiver off the rest.

He put his own back and looked at his watch. She would ring him back, of course. In the meantime he had work already piling up; Madge was pleading from her office. He'd better put her in the picture.

Meanwhile Mrs. Grosshouse had found the paperback, with its silly erotic jacket. She flapped it open at the first page of the story and read her own opening sentences, unchanged except in one small grammatical rearrangement.

She was appalled. It was *her* book, *her own words*, an open bare-faced theft! Incredible!

She turned pages, sought out passages that she knew were specially relevant to her own story. Over and over again she found them, correctly placed, cunningly changed into a modern idiom from her careful Edwardian prose. This was most obvious in the dialogue. It debased her novel to the level of all that popular trash with up-to-date morals and modern slang and cardboard characters in fancy dress.

Especially in the last part of the novel. This, she realised, in spite of the tears that had begun to flow freely, was not hers at all. It had had to be written in England while she was writing the last part of her book in Italy. There was very little correspondence with what had gone before and the plot developed to an unlikely, sentimental conclusion utterly removed from the sad, true end that was the logical conclusion of her own tale.

She turned over the last page of *The Young Adventurers*. Here was a short notice about the 'Golden Sunrise' award, an equally short paragraph about the nineteen year old west country student who had won it and a photograph of that very lovely girl herself.

"Julia Trebannon, my foot!" cried Anita Armstrong, rushing back to the telephone. "George, it's a blatant robbery, by the unprincipled baggage who did most of my typing for me!"

"Are you sure?"

It seemed so very unlikely that any girl of that age and in those far away provincial surroundings would do such a hopelessly risky thing that he found it difficult to accept.

"Of course I'm sure! My own words all the way through!"

"Really your own words?"

"Practically. Edited, I must say."

"How much edited? I mean—"

"George, don't be difficult! I'm going to ring off. I've got Ian coming down. He's read this travesty of my book. He'll accept my word for it all. Besides, there's the photograph. Goodbye!"

She rang off, tears banished, astonishment quelled, as fury grew and with it a bitter thirst for revenge.

X

The Frobishers at Minehead were worried. After their very much enjoyed holiday in Spain they had expected to see their so-called nephew Chris quite soon after their return. But he did not appear, he did not write—well, he never did write letters—he did not ring up.

This was very unusual, as Aunt Muriel said, plaintively. "We should have heard from him, if only to ask for an advance of his allowance."

Uncle Henry laughed.

"Trust Chris! I've sent the cheque to his bank as usual. I suppose he may have gone abroad himself."

"I'll write to that last address he gave us. It was a friend's flat in London, I think."

When the letter came back, address unknown, the Frobishers began to worry seriously. Who could they ask among his many friends? They realised, with a sense of shock, that they did not know the names, far less the addresses, of the many young people, boys and girls, that Chris had brought to their house for a meal, a drink—

"Several drinks," Uncle Henry remembered. "Thirsty lot, always."

"Dinners as well as lunches," Aunt Muriel added.

"Not to mention the odd fiver."

They both sighed.

90

"He was getting to be a bit of a problem," Uncle Henry acknowledged.

"He was such a sweet little boy," his aunt protested. "Never any trouble till he went to school."

They exchanged significant glances. Chris's school records were best forgotten.

"If Edgar had not been a college friend of mine and generous to us in the old days, we couldn't have kept it up," Uncle Henry concluded, boldly.

Until Muriel, startled by the frank confession, protested at this. "Edgar simply asked us if we could take him on, since he knew how we'd always wanted a family. The accountants arranged it all, didn't they?"

"That's right. No questions either side. But swore to me he wasn't his."

"I can't believe that. Could have been his sister's, though."

"No questions," Uncle Henry repeated, firmly.

After a few more weeks of patient waiting and speculation that grew more and more fanciful, the Frobishers decided they had better get public help. They appealed to the police.

Detective Inspector Rickard of the Minehead force added Christopher Trotter to the list of missing persons in the west country. He visited the Frobishers. He discovered the main facts of Chris's fostering, but the Frobishers did not mention their former friend Edgar, nor his plea for help in fostering the child. Secrecy on this matter was essential, because their comfortable income depended upon it. To the detective inspector they merely pleaded ignorance, but they did explain that the arrangement had been made privately and that expenses were paid to them by a firm of accountants, also since he came of age, an allowance for the young man, paid to him through them.

Detective Inspector Rickard found all this very meagre news. The missing boy was illegitimate, obviously, both parents unknown to the Frobishers, or so they implied. Money provided by a firm of London accountants. Well, they might disclose more, if necessary.

The Frobishers were, however, able to throw a certain amount of dim light on their foster child's present character, habits and activities. He had not trained in any profession, though he had attended a succession of courses in Plymouth. He had held a variety of jobs about the country, but mostly in London. He had a talent for art, commercial, they had gathered.

"What as?" asked Rickard. "I mean, what for?"

"I honestly don't know," Uncle Henry answered. "In various businesses, I suppose. Advertisements, perhaps. He called himself a consultant at one time. He is only twenty-nine, now."

"I see," said the detective inspector, who could make an intelligent guess. A wide boy, obviously, but not an actual villain. Not on the books, anyway not theirs. No form.

"We tried some of the hospitals," Aunt Muriel said. "In case of an accident. He always drives very fast cars."

"Does he?" said Rickard. "Where does he get them?"

"His—guardian, I suppose. I mean, the accountants who—er—reimburse our expenses—does refer to a guardian, without naming him or her. This person is very generous," Uncle Henry hastened to conclude.

"Girl friends?" asked Rickard, to rescue the other from his flounderings. "Any names?"

"Legions," said Uncle Henry.

"Any particular name?"

"Judy," Aunt Muriel was sure. "No surname. There never is. But Judy for months now, wasn't it, Harry?"

"Pretty kid, yes." Uncle Henry added, "Teenage, but very sophisticated. Student. Art and Design, wasn't it, Mu?"

"That's right. In Plymouth."

With this, the only real lead he had found in Minehead,

Detective Inspector Rickard continued his inquiries in liaison with the Plymouth force. They were reasonably productive, for they led him to get in touch with Judy Smith at the home of her parents.

The excitement that had seized the famous maritime town when it learned of the outstanding success of its junior citizen, had by now died down, giving place to its accustomed eagerness for exploits on the high seas. The troubles, fears and disputes over professional fishing usually had pride of place in local newspapers and often in the nationals as well. Local regattas throughout the sailing season had only recently come to an end. All up and down the coast from Torbay to Falmouth and beyond the small boats with their young crews never stopped competing. At another level of age and interest amateur fishing occupied the weekends of desk- or earth-bound workers. All this needed careful, knowledgeable and enthusiastic reporting. The newspaper men had therefore given up pestering the new literary lion cub. After all it was not a breed that appealed to many of their readers.

Detective Inspector Rickard who arranged his inquiries conscientiously before wasting expensive petrol, was not in the least surprised to hear from a junior woman detective constable that the Judy Smith who had been known to go about with Christopher Trotter was also Julia Trebannon, the 'Golden Sunrise' prize-winner. Juveniles these days were hogging the limelight as infant prodigies in many of the arts and on very doubtful showing, she said, as she joined him at the Smiths' home.

What did surprise them was the fact that Judy herself, while agreeing that she had gone to the Frobishers' house in Minehead several times in the spring and summer of that year, had not seen Chris at all for at least three months.

"But you say he introduced you to this publisher who took your book?"

"Yes, he did. At a party he took me to."

"Had you written it then?"

"Only partly. But he liked it, Mr. Stockley, I mean, my publisher. So I finished it."

"Did Christopher know this?"

"Oh yes. I had to go to London several times. I stayed a few times at the flat Chris had borrowed from friends who were on holiday."

"Can I have that address, please?"

Judy was prepared for this. She decided that the address of the hi-jacked flat had better be forgotten.

"You'll think me a right Charlie," she said with an embarrassed laugh, "but I've forgotten. In Chelsea, two turnings from the bus route."

As the flat had been in Fulham, she hoped it would not be traced. But she began to feel annoyed with Chris. He had certainly been out of touch; he had not come to the prize-giving, nor rung her up here at home. True she had not tried to ask him why. Actually she had not given him a thought.

"I stayed with Clare, that's my publisher's wife," she explained. "Quite a lot while I was doing the end, correcting proofs, all that—"

"And you know that address, I suppose?" asked Rickard, smiling at her. Putting on the dim girlie act, wasn't she? Pretty as a book cover, the kind his wife got every week at her super-store. But the eyes were a give-away. He'd seen them before, often, at the station, in the cells. Cold, calculating, playing it all by a keen predator's sixth sense.

A good many other people at the various college and technical institutes in Devon and west Somerset had met Chris Trotter but few had kept up their acquaintance with him, and none knew of his present whereabouts. Also it became evident that he had not appeared or at any rate had not been seen in either county for nearly three months. Just about the time his little friend Judy had made her number with her London publisher.

So the inquiries in the west country came to a discreet

end, while the name of Christopher Trotter and that of Henry with his Minehead address was circulated in the general list of missing persons.

As the season of holidays drew to an end most of those missing persons who had not told their nearest and dearest or their employers, male or female, where they had gone, either turned up again or notified in some way their intention not to return. This reduced the list of those still sought after and to some extent those whose unidentified bodies filled the seekers' descriptions. It took time but in the end a correspondence was suspected between the refrigerated young man taken from the Thames and the lost young foster-son from Minehead. In London he apparently had no police record. At Plymouth the palm-print, long stored, deemed useless, but now proving its worth, did match.

Detective Inspector Rickard went to the Frobishers' house in Minehead again, in the company of an officer from London. They saw Henry alone to explain what they had discovered and what they feared.

"Drowned!" Mr. Frobisher was appalled. "But he was a splendid swimmer! He won prizes at school."

"He had been drinking heavily, the post mortem found."

"He had a hard head, I always thought."

"No clothes on, either. The pathologist thought he must have drunk too much at a party, gone to the river to cool off and sober up and the shock of the cold water induced cramp."

The officers were interested to hear of the victim's swimming powers, but more so by Mr. Frobisher's indifference over the palm-print and over the fact that its duplicate lay in police records and had been taken from the window-ledge of an old lady in Siddicombe.

"He always was wild," Mr. Frobisher said at last, noting the expressions on the faces of the two, "and getting wilder," he added.

95

After a decent silence Rickard said, "I'm afraid it means you will have to identify him, sir."

Again Mr. Frobisher remained calm, only saying, "I'd like to tell my wife personally. She need not see the body, I hope."

"Oh no, sir," they both assured him.

Uncle Henry, moved at last by the prospect of Muriel's reaction to the news, murmured as he left the room, "Poor boy! Poor silly bastard!" Then, realising that epithet was factually correct, he was shocked at himself and stopped speaking. The two officers exchanged significant looks.

Nor did they see fit to tell that fantastically pretty girl, the prize-winning author, that her one-time boy-friend was dead. But, without warning him, they did allow the constable who looked after Siddicombe to inform old Mrs. Grosshouse that the man who had broken into her cottage had been found drowned in the Thames in London. Very little was known of him, but he seemed to have been in a fair way to becoming a regular tear-away or villain.

"Do you mean a thief? A burglar?"

"Probably. We don't know, madam." The constable saw no point in explaining the special sense of the term burglar for a night thief.

"And you don't care," the old lady said, adding, "Good riddance to bad rubbish, eh?"

The constable grinned. The old 'un obviously didn't hold with the new-fangled nonsense about sin and wickedness. He came from a God-fearing, west country dissenting family himself. He did not know that Mrs. Grosshouse was far too much upset by the theft of her novel to be interested, far less bothered, by the demise of her burglar, who had taken nothing. So she missed giving the constable some very interesting information about her part-time typist and the latter's connection with the deceased.

Mr. Frobisher went to London with the officer who had been sent down to inform and guide him. They left Mrs. Frobisher distressed, tearful, but like her husband privately relieved to hear that their growing misgivings over Chris were at an end. She withdrew into decent seclusion until Harry came back, when they were both able to agree upon their mutual relief.

"It would have been worse if it hadn't been Chris," Mr Frobisher confessed. "I must say I had qualms when they took me into the mortuary."

Mrs. Frobisher shuddered.

"Was it very awful? I know I'd have fainted."

"It was all very formal. Solemn, you know. Considerate of my feelings. Our police are truly wonderful, whatever those commy students say."

It had indeed been formal. Chris had suffered to some extent from his four or five day immersion in the polluted Thames and his journeys up and down with the tides. When they took him from his refrigerated drawer in the mortuary and laid him out on one of the slabs they covered him decently up to the neck with a spotless white sheet that hid the various discolorations that had taken place after death from impact with solid objects as well as the onset of decomposition. Fortunately the face had suffered less than other parts and the hair and beard had grown enough to hide what there had been.

Uncle Henry recognised the face without any difficulty. He agreed, with an inward shudder, that he did not wish to see more. At a police station he signed the necessary papers. There would have to be an inquest, which he must attend. But its verdict would almost certainly be accidental death. That was all for the moment, they told him, since there were no clothes or property to be handed over.

"Why not?" asked Mr. Frobisher, who had not gathered the full degradation of that drunken death.

"The body was naked when found. We have no idea

where he entered the water. But we do know he was found some distance from where he drowned."

"Someone must have found his clothes," Uncle Henry protested. "Or been looking after them, more likely. Someone, a friend, I suppose, would surely have tried to get help when he disappeared in the water."

"No one did so."

"And his money, his watch. He had a gold watch, perhaps not real gold."

"We don't know. Nicked most likely. People don't hand in valuables to the police these days. They keep them."

"Horrible. Barbarous. Back to the middle ages."

"Back to nature sir, is what we think here."

There was no answer to this. Agreeing, sighing, poor Uncle Henry went to a modest hotel to telephone Aunt Muriel and await the inquest, which took place in London.

They buried Chris in Minehead, very quietly. The local paper made as much of it as possible. A young man not yet thirty, a good swimmer, but led astray, apparently by unprincipled companions in London, that distant centre of every kind of danger, moral and physical. It might have been a car crash, driving under the influence, equally dangerous and as in this case, fatal.

At the inquest the evidence regarding the freshwater algae was not considered particularly significant. The water just above and just below Teddington was very similar. The tides ran out there faster than they ran in. The coroner chose to make little of the algae. But the police reserved their opinion on the matter.

Mr. Frobisher notified the firm of accountants who had provided the money for Chris's upbringing. He was a little surprised they had not got in touch with him themselves, since he had given their address to the police, who had no doubt been to see them about Chris. In his letter to them he had pointed out that he had paid their last cheque into

Christopher's bank account according to the arrangement he had made with the young man after he reached the age of eighteen.

He was surprised and rather indignant to be told that since the cheque had been sent after the estimated date of Mr. Trotter's death this sum was in excess of the amount due to him, but that the deceased's guardian considered that it would cover the funeral expenses, the visit to London in connection with the death and any other incidentals. They did not expect Mr. Frobisher to refund it. In fact all communication with them over the late Mr. Christopher Trotter was now at an end.

"I'm damned if it is!" Uncle Henry shouted when he had read the accountants' letter to Aunt Muriel.

"You mean that cheque doesn't cover it all?" she asked anxiously.

"By no means. I've spoken to his bank manager. He moved his account from our bank. Did you know that?"

"You never told me."

"Well, he did. First time he was overdrawn and Mr. Gibbon had a quiet word with me about it and Chris said he wasn't having that sort of dirty snooping. Only he put it more coarsely."

Aunt Muriel winced but she said only, "What did his bank manager say to that?"

"That Chris's overdraft wasn't even covered by the new cheque."

"And since then?"

"Same thing. Off and on. Usually on. Worse this last time."

"Does that mean we'll have to pay all the expenses ourselves?"

"Settle them and the overdraft out of his estate, his bank manager advises."

"But he hasn't got anything. At least nothing with us, except that old radio he gave me."

99

"No clothes, books or anything? We kept his room just as it always was, didn't we?"

For a moment the two elderly faces expressed a certain sad nostalgia, but Chris, in his culpable death, had gone too far. Too expensively so.

"Books," said Aunt Muriel, recovering her keen sense of property. "Now that reminds me. That girl of his, Judy Smith. Didn't we hear she'd won some sort of competition?"

"Beauty prize, I wouldn't wonder."

"No, no. Nothing like that. That wouldn't surprise me. No, a book she'd written. Best-seller. Under another name. Chris had something to do with finding her a publisher, I believe."

"Who told you all this fairy tale?"

"Mrs. Beacon. She's a great reader, you know."

Uncle Henry snorted. But thinking it over later, as he was giving his lawn its last mow of the year, he decided to go into it a bit further. If Chris had really had anything to do in the way of promotion with a best-selling book, then surely a commission or a percentage of the spoils was due to him. Or his heirs. Who could be only themselves unless he had made a will. Which was highly unlikely.

It was worth a try. Anything, really, to counteract the several hundred pounds he would otherwise be out of pocket. Thank God the young twister had not been his own son. Everyone knew he had not even adopted Chris.

XI

The Eve of Yesterday appeared in a modest jacket. It showed the delicately drawn picture of a late Victorian valentine.

The book was given a warm greeting by several distinguished critics and one characteristically rude notice from the most notorious among them. As Ian Macalister told Anita, who was inclined to resent the uncalled-for impertinence, "Probably does us more good than all the nice ones. Worthwhile readers want to know if he's right, so they buy it for that and to prove they're still avant-garde themselves."

"You can't possibly call my work avant-garde," she reminded him.

George, sitting on her other side, added, "Period novels are becoming very fashionable, Anita. Popular taste—"

"I know, I know, but I'm still too easily upset over this blasted book."

"You used to enjoy the rough notices more than the smooth."

"You're right, of course." She turned back to Ian. "You know I have to appear, no, I mean *speak* on that radio arts half-hour?"

He beamed at her. "I didn't, but I'm delighted."

This small restaurant literary lunch had been put on by Haseldyne to celebrate the novel's publication. The Hastons were there, also Mrs. Ford and Kate from Siddicombe, but not the vicar, who said he could not leave the parish, apart from the additional travel expenses. George Carr had brought his wife and also the representative (in London for a brief visit) of an American paperback fiction network. This individual had read and enjoyed *The Eve of Yesterday*. His firm was a rival of the one to which Len Stockley had sold *The Young Adventurers*. George had explained the blatant plagiarism involved, but the American had laughed. 'Coincidence' was the usual name for such things at home. After all, the number of basic plots was limited, wasn't it? Anyway, Miss Armstrong's novel had that true Edwardian flavour; it was bound to appeal; he catered for the more literate readership in the States and it was a growing market. He was honoured to be meeting Miss Armstrong.

Anita was delighted to be meeting the paperback king's representative. She fully understood the value of doing so. Ian, too, had briefed her about him before the luncheon.

"You mustn't startle him, Anita," he warned her. "I know George has hinted at the basic reason you had for starting to write again. You've never hidden it from us or anyone, I think."

"That is so," she answered. "I'll be all sweetness and light. Provided he doesn't call me a little old lady. But he won't have an opportunity to do that, will he?"

Ian shuddered.

"I sincerely hope not. But you never can tell with the Yanks."

"Hush! You forget I married one."

"Sorry! Apology *indeed*! Stupid ass that I am!"

"Forgiven. As long as we get the book into the States, where my fans should be. I'm sure they remember me better over there than they do here."

She was right, of course. There were many more thousands of middle-brow housewives in the States than in

102

England and the dominions put together. It was from overseas that the main part of her hoped-for gains would come. Just enough to keep on the Siddicombe home, she prayed, and Mrs. Droge and within reach of the dear Hastons.

"The reprint of *Dawn* is going quite well, too," George told her before they parted at the door of the restaurant.

"I'll see you back to your hotel," Ian said.

In the taxi he explained that it would be necessary for her to produce the original longhand manuscript of her new novel to prove the blatant plagiarism beyond any dispute.

"But I don't want you to have any trouble over it, or indeed run any risk."

"Risk of what?" she asked.

"Of the other side getting it away from you or destroying it in some way."

"It's in my bank."

"You don't know how cunning the modern criminal can be."

She was silenced by this frightful thought. All along they had told her it was such blatant plagiarism that it should not be necessary to go to the expense of taking it to court. Haseldyne was insured against loss over such things and her own liabilities for libel in any form. So there should be considerable compensation payable without a court hearing. Naturally the reaction of the enemy to that, apart from trying to prove ignorance, coincidence and so on, would be to destroy the real evidence. Which lay in her longhand, original copy of the book.

"What do you suggest?" she asked. She knew the weight of paper in bulk. She could not handle it herself. Not all the way to London. She remembered heaving the suitcase, filled with the precious stuff, into the boot of her car when she took it to the bank.

"What do you want me to do?" she asked again.

Ian had his plan quite ready. It was simple.

"I will come down with you tomorrow morning," he said.

We will drive from your house to your bank in your car, get out the manuscript—"

"It's all in the one suitcase," she interrupted.

"Fine. That makes it easy. You'll take me to the station for the next train back to London. I'll keep the suitcase in the safe at my office and our solicitors can see it and make out our case against Stockley. There'll be things for you to sign, but I don't suppose you'll have to come up again for a bit. We all want to avoid a court case, don't we?"

"Oh, yes. Indeed we do," she answered fervently.

But as she said goodbye to him in her hotel lounge, with hearty thanks for the lunch, she murmured, "But I do still resent that *prize*! Dishonest, thieving little bitch!"

The thieving little bitch was, very slowly, coming to the same conclusion. For the publicity following her triumph had, apart from her share of the lovely dough, done her more harm than good. That old deceitful cow at Siddicombe turned out to be a real author after all. Nobody had told her that, even Kate Ford. You'd have expected those church people with their private education and all to have known that. Or the librarian at the public library.

"So you had no idea that Mrs. Grosshouse was a writer?"

"None whatever. That isn't her writing name. She calls herself Anita Armstrong. I ask you!"

This was the second interview with the 'pigs', as she had learned to call them, from Feltbridge. Still making inquiries, this one said, about Chris. As if the inquest hadn't given it as an accident when drunk at a party. So why drag *her* into it? She hadn't seen him for weeks before it happened.

Detective Inspector Whimple was patient. He could not deny that his feelings in the case were not influenced by the looks of this girl, who set out her ignorance and innocence with such disarming frankness.

"I accept the fact that you thought this was an old

woman's whim you were serving. When did Mr. Trotter suggest stealing the manuscript?"

"He never!" She was outraged and showed it. Besides, in all truth, Chris really never had suggested such a thing. It had been Len.

"You thought of it yourself?"

"How dare you insult me!"

Ridiculous phrase, borrowed from television comedy or cheap journalism. Whimple smiled at her crimson fury, which he rightly judged was half acting, half genuine fright.

"Tell me how it came about, then?" he suggested.

Judy did so. Chris had taken her to a party, where she met a publisher, Mr. Stockley. They had talked about her work for Mrs. Grosshouse. She had explained that she was sorry for the old lady whose attempt to write a novel seemed to her and to the writer's housekeeper to be an attempt to make money.

"You wanted to help the old lady?" Whimple said.

They had reached this point before.

"I've told you so often and often," she answered, confirming it.

"So you are really suggesting that Chris Trotter planned your meeting with Mr. Stockley on purpose to bring this partly written novel to his attention?"

"You could say that. We wanted to help her."

"And when she left Siddicombe with Professor and Mrs. Haston, the book unfinished, you tried to discover if she had stopped writing, given it up?"

"I tried to write to her to find out, because Mr. Stockley was worried. I did write to Siddicombe to be forwarded. But I got no answer. So I suppose this Mrs. Good didn't bother to send it on."

"On the contrary Mrs. Good did send the letter on. Mrs. Grosshouse was too busy writing the last part of her novel to bother to answer it. She meant to thank you when she got back."

"Big of her," Judy said bitterly.

"In the meantime," Detective Inspector Whimple told her for the first time, "your friend Chris forced his way into Mrs. Grosshouse's cottage in Siddicombe by opening the kitchen window. He searched the place, apparently for the manuscript, because he neither took nor damaged any single thing there."

"How d'you know?" her voice had gone shrill and hard.

"Because he conveniently left his palm-print on the window sill. This was the main clue to discovering his identity."

The bloody idiot, Judy told herself, sitting very quiet and white-faced now. It was the first time she had heard the true story of the matching of that naked young corpse with Uncle and Aunt Frobisher's foster nephew.

"So it was very important to get hold of that manuscript, wasn't it?" Whimple said, pressing home the significance of what he saw clearly was news to her. "You see your famous story turns out to be a put-up job, no less."

Judy was recovering. The whole thing had been deeper than she had known. She must keep out of those depths at all costs. She repeated her basic innocence.

"I only wanted to help the old lady to get her book published and make money for her."

"But I understand you had a contract with Stockley, the publisher?"

"Yes. I did. I can show it you."

"Made out with you as the author. You did the editing, I believe, and wrote the last chapters."

"I never! I can't write! I never pretended I could. It was Len wrote them!"

"But the contract—"

"He made me sign it. I didn't want to but I didn't rightly understand what it was about. I just wanted to help Mrs. Grosshouse. I'll say that over and over."

"I'm sure you will."

Detective Inspector Whimple prepared to leave. He had

conducted his interview at the girl's home, where her mother, getting more and more impatient, had knocked at the door several times. So he signalled to the woman detective sergeant he had brought with him, they shuffled their papers together and got up to go.

"I think you may have a court case on your hands over the plagiarism," he said. "You and Mr. Stockley. But no doubt he will have his firm's solicitors on to it already. My interest is solely in the question of the death of Mr. Trotter."

"But the inquest," Judy insisted. "The verdict was accidental drowning, while—"

"Stoned. I know."

"And in the Thames. How do you come into that?"

"You'd be surprised," the Detective Inspector told her.

The Scotland Yard officer who had been such a help to poor Uncle Harry Frobisher in the disturbing matter of Chris Trotter's identification, had been following up police doubts over the manner of the drowning and the place where it had happened. The body was found between Teddington Lock and Richmond, caught up in the dead branches of trees and other rubbish at low tide. The water in the lungs and the plant life in the water were fresh, not tidal. Though the coroner had glossed over this fact, the implications were plain. Chris had either floated, or been conveyed over-land from the spot where he drowned to that where he was found.

Could he have floated? Very unlikely. He could not pass through the lock at Teddington without complicated human assistance, of which there was no evidence or indeed any likelihood. A body only a few days dead was very unlikely to have drifted over the weir without being seen unless the river was in spate, which it most certainly was not at or directly after the death. Therefore it would seem that Trotter had been moved by his friends, or were they his enemies? And if so, why?

Since all inquiries from his so-called friends and acquaintances in Devon had been reported quite negative, and the few Londoners named were equally unrewarding, the officer was left with only two lines of investigation; the one given him by the Frobishers as to the young man's parentage and the facts regarding his criminal acts which led surprisingly to the accountants who represented the background benefactor.

The accountants agreed that Chris had been difficult on more than one occasion, twice nearly tangling with the law. They were adamant in their refusal to disclose the name of the benefactor. Yes, they knew the Frobishers, an admirable pair. Yes, they paid them in quarterly cheques for the upkeep, education and care of young Trotter. Yes, since the boy came of legal age at eighteen they had added a substantial amount for him personally to be disbursed by the Frobishers to their adopted son.

"Not adopted by them, I understand," the officer said. "And nephew, not son."

In some confusion the accountants conceded these corrections. The benefactor had agreed to Mr. Frobisher's terms over the fostering while insisting upon complete secrecy over his own identity. When the officer pressed his demand to be put in direct touch with the benefactor, he met with a reappearance of the stone wall of silence. But since young Trotter had been seeing a good deal of Judy Smith the young book-prize winner, and also of her publisher, he arranged to visit Leonard Stockley, who might take a different view.

Again he met with a few facts and much frustration. Chris had introduced the young writer to him, Len agreed. He had been interested and on reading her manuscript had thought it merited publication and had given her a contract.

"In her own name?"

"Well no. In a pen name, Julia Trebannon. That sounded better. It is often done, for various reasons."

"Yes. But the book was not hers. Apparently she brought it to you at the instigation of Trotter, but it was really the work of her elderly employer."

"She brought it to me as her own work. It was not complete, but I accepted it and gave her a contract. She signed that as the author and I signed it in good faith."

"You did not suspect from her appearance and speech and so on that it was extremely unlikely she was herself capable of writing this novel? That it must be a complete plagiarism?"

"Certainly not. I am still not convinced of it, though Haseldyne are threatening—"

The officer held up a hand.

"Mr. Stockley, I am not trying to trap you into any admission over this book and its complications. I am investigating the circumstances of the death by drowning of Christopher Trotter. The circumstances, I repeat, not the manner of his death."

"But the inquest—"

The officer was about to repeat his suspicions when Clare came into the room.

"Oh, still talking?" she said, rather rudely.

"Clare!" Len protested. But the officer, who was on his feet, said, "Just going, Mrs. Stockley. Your husband has told me how Mr. Trotter introduced Miss Smith to him and why."

"*She* never wrote that book," Clare insisted. "Len was completely taken in by her. Yes, you were, Len, you can't deny it. Have you seen her, officer? Cheap glamour girl. I actually had to put her up while she was finishing that so-called novel of hers. He was taken in by her. Even Ned—"

"Clare!" yelled Len, up also by this time, struggling on

109

uncertain feet towards her. "Hold your tongue, You silly lying—"

The officer, stepping between them, said quickly to Clare, "Who is Ned? Tell me at once."

"Ned? Don't you know? Hasn't he told you? The man who put him into publishing—"

"He didn't! It was you made me try it. Ned was good enough to help. My kind and helpful backer, now rewarded, thank God."

"And we all know why."

She was frantic. The pent-up jealous anger and hatred over the whole business of this miserable book; the suspicion; the temporary astonished joy in an overflowing bank balance, so swiftly turned into despair and ruin; all this was too much for her shallow self-centred being. To Len's horror she gave away various details of his shady business transactions that he had not imagined she could possibly know. She knew far too much about Ned and spoke it all, calling him by his full name, which the police officer wrote down with satisfaction.

When at last Clare came to an end of her tirade, her hysteria emptied out of her for the time being, she had not enough strength to do more than collapse into a chair and fumble for a handkerchief. It was Len who took the officer to the front door, saying, without bitterness, "I am sure you will discount most of that outburst. My poor wife does not know what she's saying when she has one of these attacks. Later on she will be sorry and full of shame and remorse."

"Quite so, sir," the officer said and left quickly.

The Young Adventurers was withdrawn from the libraries and bookshops, while *The Eve of Yesterday* took its place, achieving a good deal of demand as news of the suspected plagiarism was spread abroad by the media.

For the present nothing was done about the great pile of early editions of *The Young Adventurers*, beyond suspend-

110

ing the printing of the fourth edition. But a very large printing of the paperback edition in English went to the binders on the way to full production and in several foreign countries paperback translations continued to be bought and sold.

In Plymouth Mr. Smith encouraged his daughter Judy to buy a boat for her pleasure that he could also use for fishing. His old fishing boat, he told her, was getting too old for safety; she had leaked badly this season and her engine was really beyond repair.

"You can well afford it, my girl," he told her. "And you've always liked going out with me, haven't you, love?"

She agreed with that. Besides, she rather fancied herself as a yachtswoman and owner of her own craft. So with her dad's help she bought a neat little cabin cruiser, seaworthy, almost new, proved by two seasons in Torbay and thereabouts. To show her independence she secured a mooring in Dartmouth and took her family and friends out to sea for short trips. Nobody told her that the trim little vessel might be forfeit if the plagiarism case went against her.

XII

Len Stockley was left in no doubt whatever that his benefactor and patron was not only disappointed by the blow that had fallen on *The Young Adventurers*, he was furious. He was also, though he dared not admit it, even to himself, very frightened. He had always felt that Len was unreliable, though hitherto he had had his uses. But this showed him to be more than unreliable; he was dangerous.

"You have deceived me from the start of this business!" he roared at him. "You're a bloody liar!"

"No. No! I swear I told you what I thought was the truth. You must believe me! It was Chris lied to you. Every time. I swear—"

"You make me sick!"

Len had been called to Ned's London flat after he had been forced to explain why there was this fuss over the prize-winning book. Part of Ned's anger lay in the fact that he knew next to nothing about books or the writers of such things. As a self-made man, who had risen from very humble beginnings, he had found no time in his scramble for wealth, for position, for the rewards of a grateful government, to indulge himself, or rather waste his time, upon any of the arts. As Sir Edgar Seven he was well on the way to further honours, he believed. And if some of his business transactions would be frowned on pretty heavily in high

112

places, well, surely with his amazing shrewdness and knowledge of the world, what was there to fear?

The shock of finding an abyss at his feet, an opening split there by his ignorance, his own total ignorance, of the world of books, terrified him. His vanity, his self-confidence, were shrivelled suddenly. He suffered more than he had done at any time since his school days, when the fights with those he had cheated or robbed had not always gone in his favour.

"Call yourself a publisher!" he went on more quietly, but with increased scorn. "Call yourself a publisher and never heard that old woman was already an author. Let alone knew she'd done a best-seller in her day."

"She wasn't Mrs. Grosshouse when she wrote *Too Late for the Dawn Chorus*. She was Anita Armstrong, the name she uses for this new book Haseldyne have just published."

"The book you nicked. The book you've landed me with."

"I didn't nick it. It was Chris. He dreamed up this crazy scheme. He introduced me to Judy. She brought the manuscript—as her own work."

"Are you trying to tell me you didn't know she's incapable of writing anything on her own? Because Chris told me the truth there. I'm pretty sure of that. He got her into the game as an idea he sold her of helping the old woman to make money. I'm ready to believe that. It was up to you to know it wasn't Mrs. G's senile attempt. You could have asked round a bit, couldn't you? Before you gave the girl a contract. Bogus, as it turns out. Call yourself a publisher!"

"I never have called myself a publisher!" Len cried. "I was a journalist, you know that. It was Chris made it sound a good move. Chris and Clare between them. You'd put money into it and a regular supply —"

Ned's hard palm cut across his face, knocking his lips against his teeth and his teeth against his tongue. He choked, shuddered, fumbled for a handkerchief to check

113

the blood that had already fallen on his shirt, then moaning lay back in his chair while his patron, his savage patron, moved away to the window and stayed there, his back turned, looking out.

At last Ned said slowly, "Chris was very much to blame. He was out for himself, always. But he's gone, so you'll leave him out of this and every other matter concerning him."

He was speaking now as he might have done in arranging a course of action for one of his many business activities. Solway, Seven Export Consultants Limited. The ever successful consultants. The firm limited to himself, for he was Solway too, all the shares he held personally.

He turned slowly from the window but did not go back to his own chair. Instead he moved towards Len, noting with satisfaction that the feeble idiot shrank a little lower at his approach.

"There will be no court case," he said. "You will agree that the thing was a what-d'you-call-it."

"Plagiarism," Len murmured, trying to retrieve some remnant of self respect.

"That, then," Ned went on. "No case and compensation payable out of the fortune you're making. Put the blame on the girl if you can and as much as you can. Join her with the compensation."

"The prize was paid to her direct."

"Then she'll be well able to help with the compensation."

"There'll be no more sales, unless there's a settlement. Our only excuse is coincidence. No one will wear that, I don't mind betting. The libraries and bookshops have to withdraw *The Young Adventurers* from their shelves."

Ned stared. Why had he ever tried to use this hopeless creature. *His* bookshops? *His* shelves! *His* printers! *His* binders!

"I tell you. Are you listening, Len? There will be no court

114

case. The old woman needs money, so she won't want to see her compensation sliding into the lawyers' pockets. As for you, if you have to be wound up it only serves you right. You can carry that can, too."

Len was beyond argument, beyond protest. He knew he was finished. He could still taste the blood in his mouth, he knew that both his tongue and lips were swollen, he would have to go home in a taxi. All right, he was finished. There would be no more supplies from this source so he would swallow those reserves he had hidden for years and Ned could hear of his death just before or just after the Law got his last message.

His manner changed, as it always did upon the rare occasions when he resolved on a line of action. He struggled to his feet.

"All right," he said. "No court case. A full description of how Chris dreamed up the production of this novel, using the girl. Your consent to it, confirming me in my undertaking to publish. Your suggestion that we enter it for the Golden Sunrise competition. My agreement against my doubt that the girl had really written the book. More likely Chris. But you can't produce him now, to deny or confirm, can you?"

His little burst of courage was fading away like the last spurts of flame on a fire too readily damped down with slack. He dared not finish the threat he had set out to deliver a minute before. That Chris's death had been convenient, in fact necessary. That Ned had somehow contrived it, but in the outcome, clumsily. For as with the prize the entry was dangerously over-confident, so was the nakedness of the dead Chris, to conceal identity.

Ned took the whole of Len's diatribe for its true worth, its conclusions unclear, its import for his own danger, negligible. He moved to his house telephone and ordered his own car to the door.

"You seem to be out of your mind," he said, "and you

hurt your mouth when you tripped and fell against my heavy desk. So I am sending you home in the car. Give my love to Clare. I will send you the usual packet before the end of the week."

Len lay back on the rear seat of the Rolls with his eyes closed, weak tears escaping slowly from under the wrinkled lids.

Clare Stockley's response to the new development over *The Young Adventurers* was predictable. All her past experience of her husband had taught her only one thing, his utter failure to earn his living, their joint living. His prospects had always been splendid. The outcome bitter disappointment. Each attempt he had made to build himself a reputation had collapsed in ruin. No editor wanted his articles; they had been written too late, or too early. They had offended this group or that; they were too stark or too florid. His old friends had melted away from affectionate frequent contact to the safety of a few words on a yearly Christmas card.

So when the amazing news of the best-selling novel, shouting long sought success in quite unbearably loud accents; when money poured into the joint bank account, extinguishing the overdraft for the first time in their marriage, Clare felt inclined to go on her knees to a vague, only half believed in Creator, in gratitude and also in remorse for her persistent unkindness to the man she had once loved.

This mood was still upon her when he arrived, very late, from the London house of his patron. She had not heard the Rolls draw up, and at once drive away again. But she did hear him in the hall, fumbling with the door, pushing across the chain; she did hear his slow, uncertain steps as he moved from the front door to the sitting room. So she was on her feet when he stood on the threshold, holding his scarf across the lower part of his face with one hand while he reached for the nearest chair with the other. Failing to

116

find its support he slid to his knees and then to the floor.

This was enough. Back to standard form, back to the inevitable theme song. Ruin, ruin, it's all gone wrong. Ruin, dreary ruin.

Without bothering to ask for details of his deplorable state she applied the usual remedies. Long ago Ned had told her about Len's mild addiction. He was stabilised, she was told. Much would depend upon herself to keep him from exceeding his routine. So far he had submitted to her as he might have done to his doctor.

So now she got him to the sofa near the fire. She gave him his 'fix', she covered him with a rug, she set about bathing his face. To ask for an explanation would, she knew, be useless. But she determined to keep him in bed the next day and to visit their bank manager in the morning.

It was not until the following evening that Len managed, in spite of a continued difficulty and pain over speech, to tell her exactly what had happened in his interview with Sir Edgar.

"Blood-sucking old shark," she exclaimed when he spoke of the compensation his patron demanded. "Isn't he filthy rich? Didn't he encourage you to publish the book?"

"More or less ordered me to do it."

"Did you tell him Judy didn't really write it?"

"He knows now. Deceitful little cat."

"Oh come off it, darling. You knew all along."

It was so like her response on so many other occasions, so tolerant, with the old familiar endearment, that he caught and held her close, speechless, miserable, pleading silently for forgiveness.

"We'll fight, won't we?" Clare said. "Surely there's enough money to pay him back, without taking our last penny?"

"I don't know. He was beside himself. I've never seen him quite like that before. When he hit me—"

She nodded.

117

"I suppose that's why he hasn't rung up to ask if you're all right?"

"I suppose so. He was so furious it was almost as if he was frightened."

"*Frightened! Ned!* Impossible. What about?"

"I had just mentioned Chris. The inquest—"

"Oh, that. No, he couldn't be frightened about that. An accident. Chris wasn't a junky, was he?"

"Quite the opposite, I always thought."

"Then how did he know Ned was supplying you? And others, I suppose?"

"He might have. Blackmail and Ned got rid of him."

She was genuinely shocked by this idea.

"You weren't such a fool as to let him think you were suggesting such a thing?"

"Of course not. I'm not out for suicide."

He remembered his often repeated longing for oblivion, comparing it with his present mood of reckless hope.

They stared at each other, less concerned now with the failure of Leonard Stockley, publisher, than with the real nature of their obligation to Sir Edgar Seven, tycoon, consultant exporter and importer.

After a pause Clare said, "Oughtn't you to see Judy about all this? She's at home in Plymouth, isn't she? Have you heard from her?"

"I did have a card. From Dartmouth. She went there with her father to buy a cabin cruiser with her prize money."

"A *what*?"

"Boat. Her father likes fishing. Always took her with him as a child. Been advising her, it seems. With an eye to using her little cruiser for himself, I expect."

Clare said, her eyes brightening, "We must talk to her before the lawyers take her boat from her. Shall I ask her up to stay for a weekend?"

He looked at her, trying to smile, but unable to make his swollen lips respond.

"Yes. Do that," he agreed. "I'd like to know how she stands now. Sure to blame it all on me, of course. But I'm right to withhold royalties until I know how the case will go. Naturally I've had to put it all on her."

"You old rogue!"

It was unexpected, embarrassing. An expression, affected, Edwardian, he would never have thought possible from ultra-up-to-date Clare. It was true, of course. He knew that in the end, some time when he was unhazed by his prop, his life-line, he would feel the impact of his own degradation, he would look up from the bottom of that well of infamy to the small circle of clear brightness—.

Even now, Len checked the extravagance of his unspoken words, he felt only contempt for his habitual fantasy. But Clare must have conceived some way of escape for them and it must involve Judy. He did not want to see the girl again, ever. But if Clare could use her she was entitled to try.

So Judy, wondering, curious, but wary, went to London again, to listen to Clare's plan and to make up her own mind on its feasibility.

They would take her new boat, Clare said, for a cruise to the Mediterranean, to avoid the awfulness of the English winter, now so nearly upon them. They need not sail the long, hard way all round Spain. She had heard from friends you could go across France from Bordeaux by canal. But they need not even attempt the west coast of France. They could reach the canals from the Channel coast. And they could leave the boat at some point to make their way to Switzerland and there deposit all the suspended money from the book in a secret account until they found a way to take it and themselves to some haven still further off.

In the meantime, Clare said, forestalling Judy's natural question, she would contact an old friend of an aunt of hers who would provide a loan or put them up.

"Where?" Judy asked, not believing that this character existed.

"The Dordogne."

Judy listened to further explanation, still incredulous, but with caution, showing a reluctant agreement. According to a solicitor in Plymouth, who had confessed that he knew very little about the penalties of plagiarism, she, as well as Len, would be liable to pay a large amount of compensation, over and above settling all the expenses of production, most of which had been provided by the mysterious friend and patron called Ned.

"What about this backer of yours, this feller called Ned?" she asked, turning from the voluble Clare to the silent publisher. "Won't he want his money back?"

"He's stinking rich," Clare said, quickly forestalling her husband. "Very big business. Export and import. He wouldn't miss it. A drop in the ocean."

"He might not miss it," Judy said, who knew better, "but he might mind, all the same."

"He's hopping mad already," Len could not help blurting out.

Clare looked furious, Judy said nothing. But she thought the plan was a mad one and she decided that she could not agree until she had at least consulted this man, Ned, because if he agreed to it he would know exactly how it could be done, and if he did not agree they had better not try it.

The problem was how to get in touch with the tycoon. Len had never allowed her to meet him, nor, as far as she knew, had Ned ever asked Len to present her. But once or twice, while she was staying with the Stockleys during the last stages of writing *The Young Adventurers*, Len had driven her into the City and stopped outside a tall building where the offices of the occupants were written up on a long brass plate just inside the entrance. There were about ten names of companies whose offices were located on the five floors of the building. She would have to discover where this building lay and which name belonged to the prosper-ous Ned. Clare had refused both name and address. So had Len.

It was not an impossible task, but might take time. She therefore put off her decision over Clare's plan, she told her, until she had talked to Len's lawyer, who was conduct-ing the correspondence with his opposite number working for the other publisher Haseldyne.

At first she got nothing from this man, but when she referred to visits with Len to a place in the City, implying that she knew it well, he asked, surprised, if she meant Solway, Seven Limited in Barbecue Street? She said yes, agreed that Len was in touch there, and shortly afterwards left.

Arriving in Barbecue Street by taxi, she walked along slowly. It was a narrow street, darkened by the rows of tall buildings on either side. But her task was made easier by this, for she could read most of the names showing in different ways near the doors or on bleak, paint-washed windows of the ground floors. She completed her search on one side and turned back, crossing the street to the opposite pavement. It was as she reached the kerb that she had to jump forward to escape a taxi that was just drawing up beside her. The car behind it in this one-way thoroughfare swung out to pass, the driver cursing Judy whom he con-cluded had forced the taxi's action. The girl was indignant, but rapidly forgot the insults when she saw that the two people who were paying off the taxi were the Frobishers, from Minehead, whom she knew as Chris's Uncle Henry and Aunt Muriel.

The meeting was a tremendous surprise to them all. Especially as they discovered they were looking for the same block of offices.

Uncle Henry said, "Mu, why don't you and Judy find somewhere to have a cuppa? Unless you have an appoint-ment, Judy?"

"No, she answered. "I was just walking around exploring. The firm of Solway, Seven had something to do with my publisher, Leonard Stockley. You know Len, don't you?"

Seeing their faces, she said, "I'm so sorry. I forgot. It was poor Chris took him—and me—to meet you at Minehead, wasn't it?"

"That's right," Uncle Henry said. "Come back here in half an hour, both of you. I'll be through by then and we might have a bit of lunch together."

Aunt Muriel said nothing just then, but later, sipping coffee at a small shop round the corner of Barbecue Street, she said far too much.

Judy learned, with some surprise and great enlightenment, that Chris had gone to the Frobishers when three months old to be fostered, not adopted.

"It was gratitude on Harry's part, because Sir Edgar had been good to him. They were at college together and Ned had been more successful than Harry in business. But he set us up, partly in the business, partly by paying for Chris's upbringing. That was chiefly why we didn't adopt, only fostered, you understand."

Judy did understand. In business matters she was in no way deficient.

"So who was Chris really?" she asked. "This Sir Edgar's?"

"Sir Edgar Seven, dear. No, not his son. He's never married. But I believe his sister's, though why she didn't get rid of it—well that was never our business, you understand."

Again Judy understood.

"I suppose you told Chris who he was when he grew up?" she said.

"No. Never." Aunt Muriel was agitated.

"But I'm sure he knew."

"We never told him. He wasn't to know. We promised."

122

"He did know," Judy was positive. "Chris made him look after Len. Chris made me help Len, too. All this business over the book—"

Judy stopped herself. She was beginning to talk too much. Aunt Muriel had talked too much, far too much. That was certain. They had better both stop.

"*Chris!*" said Aunt Muriel, fumbling for her handkerchief. "He was a sweet little boy," she whispered.

XIII

When Judy had seen the Frobishers reunited outside the office block, had taken leave of them and watched them hail a taxi and were driven away, she went through the entrance, found the lift and had herself conveyed to the floor where Solway, Seven Limited operated their business affairs.

She had refused Uncle Henry's renewed offer of lunch. He did not seem to mind; in fact from his expression she guessed that his interview with the benefactor had not been a pleasant one. She was beginning to understand why.

Sir Edgar was engaged, she learned, and did not give interviews except by appointment. If she would state her name and reason for calling it might be possible towards the end of the week.

"I shall not be in London by the end of the week," Judy said roughly. She was beginning to resent the manner of this grey-haired old faggot at the reception desk.

"What name is it?" The musical voice had not altered. The elegant grey hair-do and discreet, well-cut town suit were a reproach to Judy's new, expensive, tasteless casuals. She gave her pen name, Julia Trebannon, said her business was urgent and did not fail, by her expression, to show triumph when the woman got up hurriedly and went away without another word.

She came back after an interval so long that Judy's attitude of defiance had slackened and with it her nerve.

"Sir Edgar can spare you ten minutes now," the woman said. "Come with me, please."

Quaking inwardly, Judy was nevertheless determined not to be thrown by these preliminaries. To hell with Sir Edgar Seven. He was only Ned, wasn't he? Chris's old foster-parents' bank booster, Len's backer? The man with the ready?

The room was large, the window wide, with the usual view of roofs, endless, ugly. The fabulous Ned rose from behind a large flat-topped desk, not very tall, not very old. Seemingly quite ordinary, Judy thought. Certainly very friendly as he came forward to shake hands with her.

It was all very disarming. She had come with every intention of defending her absolute right to keep the money she considered she had earned, backed by Aunt Frobisher's indiscreet disclosures. But she felt her power of attack fading as she was led by a gentle hand to a chair near the wide desk.

"My dear Miss Trebannon," Sir Edgar said, going back to his own seat. "I can quite understand your present worry. I do happen to know you are staying with the Stockleys. I would have thought Len had put you fully in the picture."

"He can't," she said bluntly. "As far as I know you've only been told lies about this bloody book."

Sir Edgar did not even blink. He only smiled, which sent a little shiver down Judy's back, but otherwise increased her determination to fight him.

"He'll have told you I wrote it and he just liked it and wanted to publish it and so you helped him."

"I liked it too," Sir Edgar said. "Very much. It seemed to me to be just what I wanted for him."

His manner continued to puzzle and annoy the girl. But she had to make him understand.

125

"He did all the end part himself," she insisted. "I only had to alter the words a bit, more up to date, you know."

As there was still no response she went on with growing desperation. "It was Chris at the start. It was his idea, to help old Mrs. Grosshouse get money from the book being published. So that was how I was hooked on making the extra carbons, right?"

"Chris was a friend of yours, Len tells me," Sir Edgar said. Judy remembered that Aunt Muriel had not meant to tell her so much about the dead boy. She did not have any grudge against the Frobishers on Chris's account so she decided not to disclose her fresh knowledge.

She said, "Ya, he was a friend ever since he began taking the arts course. He did drawings for adverts, gent's suits and that. Didn't you know?"

She got no answer to this so she went on, "He told me, quite often, he nicked things. He didn't say what, but I always wondered where he got the bread, I mean the money, to take me to the places we had meals. Specially here in London. Slap-up restaurants and that. Never in trouble. Not Chris, poor bloody sap."

"You thought him reckless, then?"

"Well, I ask you. Getting himself drowned and mugged into the bargain, before or after. The coroner was way off the beat, wasn't he?"

"I'm not in a position to know. Perhaps you may be. But tell me, Miss Trebannon, why exactly you want to consult me now and what about."

So she told him. About the prize money and her purchase of a motor cruiser. About her frozen royalties and Len's explanations, that did not ring true. About the open abuse and suspicion at the college, when news of the plagiarism attack got out, with all its attendant speculation. About the reports that Mrs. Grosshouse was out for blood.

"She could be darned insulting if you annoyed her," Judy

126

explained. "Snob voice, sarky. I'd of walked out on her if I hadn't needed the lolly."

"Are you suggesting I should take some part in trying to placate this woman for the theft of her book?"

"No!" Judy was both horrified and surprised at the idea. Spread her obligations? No and NO again! She said in a strangled voice, breathless, "Never! You must believe me, never!"

"My poor child," said Sir Edgar, smiling more widely than ever, "You must think I am some sort of an ogre. I only want to help in this matter. Both the Stockleys and you, yourself."

Temporarily soothed, Judy told him all about Clare's plan and the royalties and Switzerland and the cabin cruiser as the innocent-seeming way of escape.

"Do you know enough about managing boats to undertake such an adventure?" Sir Edgar asked.

"Oh yes. I've been out and around with Dad for years, fishing."

"You would need charts. And passports. And visas if you attempted America."

They both laughed. So he was neither shocked nor surprised. Neither did he offer approval or rebuke. An odd character, she thought. A bit spooky?

A buzzer sounded on his desk. He pressed a button and listened, his head bent over the buzzer. Judy could not hear the message but understood it only when he got to his feet.

"My next appointment," he said. "I must send you away. But I'll think over what you have told me."

"I only want to keep my prize," she said. "Len ought to pay if anyone does."

"We'll see how it all falls out," he told her, taking her elbow to guide her to the door. The pressure was unnecesary. But she found it soothing.

"You'll be with the Stockleys a little longer?"

127

"Until we hear if the lawyers have made a settlement, as they call it."

"I see. I'll get in touch then."

He did not say how, nor did she ask. She found herself passed swiftly to reception, to the lift, to the street. She wondered what good, if any, she had done herself by forcing that curious interview. But at any rate she had met Sir Edgar Seven, Ned. She knew she had never met his like before in her life. That was strange, unnerving, but most exciting. She did not tell Len and Clare of her visit to the City: nor did she mention the Frobishers. Ned had been at college with Uncle Henry, had he? Which college had that been? Oxbridge? Never! Perhaps Borstal? She giggled at her own wit, but disclaimed it with a savage curse at herself and then at the memory of her drowned boy friend. All his fault. Or no, partly her own for trying to move too quickly up that ladder to wealth that she was determined to climb.

The invitation from Sir Edgar came by special messenger in a very ordinary brown envelope, sealed. Judy was alone in the Stockleys' Hampstead house, so the implied secrecy or merely the avoidance of outrageous postage, was unnecessary. The note inside the envelope was typed.

Dear Miss Trebannon,

       I am having a small informal evening party on November 10th. I hope you will be able to come. It will be held at my country house from 7.30 p.m.

Yours sincerely,
E. F. Seven.

Buffet supper.
Swimming.

R.S.V.P. to
Meadowside,
Nr. Sunningdale,
Bucks.

The signature was a stamped facsimile. Judy wondered what the F. stood for. Should she reply as requested; she had met these four letters very often of late on other invitations; ought it to be to Sir E. F. Seven or to Sir Edgar Seven? She was calling him Ned in her mind because Len and Chris had always called him that. Obviously the answer, her acceptance, must go to the Bucks address, where he would always be known as Sir Edgar, surely.

Buffet supper, was it? No trouble there. Swimming? In November? Heated pool, she supposed. Well, not for her, thank you. Not that it would make much difference to what she wore under her dress. She would consult Clare. She and Len must have been to old Ned's informal parties and would know what they were like.

But that evening when they were sipping their coffee after dinner, Judy decided to say nothing about her invitation. She had remembered in detail the lies she had told Ned about the publisher. Clearly they had not been asked to the party and it would at best annoy them to think that she was going, and at worst they would suspect her of intrigue. They did not know of her visit to the City. The Frobishers were not likely to be in touch with them: they must be back in Somerset by now.

So, wearing her best separate long skirt and lurex-threaded tunic and her gold strapped cork-based sandals, and with a deep-fringed shawl to keep out the seasonal chill in the air, Judy set off to travel by bus and tube to Waterloo and by train to Sunningdale. She started early because she had no idea how far she was going from London, nor how long the journey would take. Besides, she wanted to get to Sunningdale well before any other possible London guests. It would be embarrassing to have to acknowledge her total ignorance to people who would recognise her later. It would be much better to get there first, take a taxi and make suitable excuses to old Ned if she got to his place far too early.

Certainly at Sunningdale there were no other likely look-ing travellers, only a couple of housewives, exhausted by a day's London shopping, piling into cars their husbands had brought down to the station for them. And four busi-nessmen who had travelled early to avoid the worst of the rush hour. They had their own cars in the station park.

There were no taxis on the forecourt. After waiting for ten minutes Judy went inside to the ticket office.

"I really want a taxi," she said, as the clerk waited for her to state her needs. "A taxi to take me to a house called Meadowside near here," she added, as the young man looked blank.

"It's Sir Edgar Seven's house," she went on, beginning to feel desperate.

"Oh, *him*." The clerk looked her up and down. "Calls his place Meadowside, does he?"

"I want a taxi," Judy repeated, becoming angry.

The clerk, catching the eye of a potential customer, who was waiting patiently behind the girl, said, "Yes, sir, where to?" then looking at Judy added, "Sorry, love, no regular rank. But they come in."

It was now nearly half-past six and she knew that the rush hour in central London must have passed its thousands into all the suburban trains. She hurried outside again and as she did so a car turned into the forecourt. It did not have any mark to show its nature but she was used, at home in Devon, to all manner of vehicles that plied for hire at stations on the main lines, so she signalled to the new-comer.

The car circled the forecourt and came to rest beside her.

"Taxi?" she asked in a shrill voice above the noise of the engine that the driver had not switched off.

"Where to, miss?"

She gave him the address, at which information he looked dubious, screwing up his mouth.

"Best part of four miles. Cost you a lot."

"How much?"

"Best part of two quid, I reckon."

"O.K. But I'm not going to pay you till we get there."

He grinned at her.

"Hop in, love."

He waited until she had slammed the rear door of the car, then started away with a jerk that threw her back on the seat. It must be a taxi, she decided, because it had four doors. An old-fashioned, four-door saloon, owner driver, probably. Though she felt doubts rise from time to time as they travelled, particularly when she noticed the two-way radio on his dashboard and heard him speak briefly into it, she still thought maybe he had a partner or an office to relay calls. He had spoken more like an employer than a servant.

Meadowside, floodlit, was exactly the sort of house she had expected, large, redbrick, wide windows, not old, not modern, a short drive and a wide sweep up to the house, three white steps before the front door. There were several cars parked there already.

Unexpectedly, quite suddenly, Judy felt shyness throw a sticky pall over her. It was unexpected, which made it all the more disturbing.

"How much?" she asked, leaning forward, not moving towards the door.

"One seventy-five, miss."

She gave him two pound notes.

"Keep the change. I was lucky you came." She still hesitated, then characteristically took action.

"Look," she said. "I don't really know this bloke or his friends. I may not want to stay long. I don't know how I'll get back to the station."

"Won't Sir Edgar give you a lift, or one of his pals?"

"You know who lives here, then?"

"Everyone in Sunningdale knows that, miss."

"I suppose they do. I just wondered,—could you call back for me in say a couple of hours, to take me back to the station. There's a train I plan to get at nine-thirty. Could you?"

He'll think me a right Charlie, acting like I never went to parties, little-girl-wet-her-pants type.

But the taxi driver got out of his seat, went round to open the door for her, gave her a hand as she climbed out, bunching up her long skirt and said casually, "Sure, I'll be back. Don't you worry. Couple of hours, did you say?"

"That's right. I'll just tell them I've booked a taxi and not to worry. If they ask."

From the moment she was welcomed by Sir Edgar and passed from group to group by willing, even eager, young men, Judy's shyness left her. Most of the other guests were the sort of people she had been meeting ever since the prize-giving. Business people, stodgy men and smart women with tightly moulded heads of hair in many unnatural colours and make-up that tried unsuccessfully to cover the advance of time, but could not cure, however careful the green shadow, the fading of dim eyes, nor the tiny creases at their corners.

True, there was a certain number of young people present and Judy was pleased to see that the costume she wore was clearly correct in every particular. All the girls were in some form of long skirt narrow or full, with either a blouse or a tunic top. Sir Edgar and the older men wore dinner jackets. The boys' clothes were as casual as those of the girls, but there were no jeans, no frayed trouser ends, no heavy sweaters. Beards were few and trimmed where present.

For about an hour and a half the company milled about in three large ground-floor rooms. Judy never discovered who, if anyone, was acting as hostess. But the company seemed not to bother with formalities of any kind. She had no trouble in finding, or rather being supplied with, plate-fuls of really delicious food, served cleverly for eating direct in the hand from plastic plates.

132

There was also a very copious supply of wine. At first Judy drank thirstily. The journey had been worrying, demanding; relief made her relax too fast. But she was always careful over drink, always had been and this was no exception.

By half-past eight the in-flowing of guests had stopped, the supper plates were empty and the word went round that swimming was now the order of the day.

"Where?" Judy demanded of the two young men who were at that moment beside her and moving her slowly towards an open french window.

The night came gently through it, but it was a chill air, seasonally sharp, and she pulled her shawl close, wrapping her hands in it.

"The swimming pool, of course," they told her and seeing her still blank look of inquiry, one of them explained.

Sir Edgar had made a natural swimming pool out of a little inlet from the river. It was so constructed that the entry was bricked over to make a sort of culvert which could be shut off to keep the water in when the Thames was low in a hot summer, and prevent the surrounding concrete border from flooding when the river rose after much rain. Moreover the pool was roofed in and could be heated.

"Come and see," they said. "You needn't swim if you don't fancy it."

"Not likely!" Judy answered, but she went with them all the same.

She had not realised, driving there along dark, tree-lined lanes, lit by occasional street lamps, with stretches where only the taxi's headlights showed the road, that Meadowside was actually on the river; 'Thames' side', it should have been called. Her young companions' description was correct, she found. Already several men and girls were splashing in the water and did not seem to be put off by the cold.

133

The water might be heated, she thought, but the air, even under the transparent roof, was not. Looking up she saw a pale moon, distorted into a blurred oblong shape. Some concealed lighting did more to obscure than enlighten the pool or the bathers.

Almost at once Judy found herself beside Sir Edgar.

"Not changed yet," he said. "I thought you were a famous swimmer."

How did he know she'd won a couple of local prizes at the Plymouth regatta, she wondered. It made her uncomfortable. This old goat, stinking rich, always knew too much. Her early shyness or reluctance or uncertainty, whatever it was, came upon her again, but she found her host compelling. With reluctance she went into the nearest changing cubicle, which she found empty. But before she left Sir Edgar a manservant in a white jacket with a tray of round-bodied brandy glasses had halted beside them and the tycoon insisted upon her joining him in a glass.

"Warm you up for the plunge," he had told her as she moved away, glass in hand.

When she reached the seclusion of the cubicle she poured the brandy on to the tiled floor and knew that getting rid of it had been one good reason for her submission. Still uncertain, still unwilling, she took off her long skirt and her lurex top and slipped out of her clumsy big sandals. Underneath she had merely her pants and a small bra. It was not really a bikini, but in this dim light would serve for one. She hid her handbag in the folds of her skirt and went out to the pool.

Sir Edgar was still standing just outside; the waiter with the tray was still beside him. The pool was full of people now, bouncing about, playing with a ball, trying to dive, after shouting for a clear space.

Judy felt less and less inclined to join them. She knew nobody. Even the young men who had chatted her up indoors had vanished.

"Have another," Sir Edgar ordered and the waiter moved forward.

"No thanks. I have a pretty long journey home," she answered, fending off the tray.

"We'll see you home, my dear."

Bemused, resentful, she found herself with a glass in her hand. The waiter moved off.

"Drink up. Drink up," Sir Edgar insisted.

It was then that she panicked. The edge in his voice, the strange insistence, meaningless, but menacing. She remembered taking a look at her watch as she slipped it into her handbag. After nine and she had asked that taxi to be back at nine. She must go. She must *go*! To hell with swimming.

"All right," she said, in a low, fierce whisper. "All right, you bloody old bully! I don't *want* to swim. Why *should* I?" she lifted her hand and flung the brandy straight at her host's face.

He saw what she intended in time to dodge the stinging fluid, but it fell between them and as he took a step forward to grab at the glass still in her hand he slipped on the brandy and stumbled. Judy, jumping sideways, pushed the bulk looming between her and the edge of the pool. He was off his balance; he fell in, flat on, fully clothed and winded by the impact.

In the next second three young men, wearing trunks, dived into the water from their positions among the surrounding bushes and went to the rescue at a brisk crawl, ploughing their way between, over and under the startled crowd.

Judy's childish panic turned to horror. But this cooled her. She had sometimes, with Chris, been at discotheques where groups or gangs operated. What she had just seen was reminiscent. As she dragged herself into her garments, flung her shawl over her head and shoulders and snatched up her bag and sandals, her single thought, her wits fully alert, was to leave this place while the uproar continued to grow, as it had done second by second from the moment Sir Edgar's considerable bulk hit the water.

Nobody saw her slip from the changing cubicle, dart behind it and finding a narrow path there among the bushes follow it in the direction of the house. It led to a wider path, gravelled, through a formal pergola where late roses still hung, sad shrivelled roses and buds already touched by frost. They caught in her shawl and her hair and tore at her hands as she pulled them away. But she did not stop until she found herself emerging on to the well-kept grass beside the drive.

The pale moon gave some light, but the floodlighting was out, she saw with thankfulness. Some of the parked cars were still there. She wondered vaguely where the rest were, for surely most of that crowd had come in their own transport. As she stepped quickly into her sandals she looked about her, searching for the taxi, which should be waiting. She found no sign of it, but realised, cursing herself, that she had not really registered its make in her mind, nor taken note of its number.

She fumbled in her handbag for her watch, her new, expensive, tiny gold watch and bracelet. Clare's taste and persuasion against her own cruder inclination.

Yes, it was after the time she had ordered and he wasn't there. Then, one of these cars that was unlocked and had its key in the dashboard. She began her search.

She was interrupted by a flash of headlights in the road and stood back to watch. Yes, it was a stopping car, not a passer-by. In her excitement she began to run towards the entrance, to be brought up sharply erect as the bonnet swung round and the light fell fully upon her.

Before she had time to put up a hand the light faded and the car retreated into the road, Judy following. She found the front passenger door already open. She jumped in. As she did so, the house floodlights came on again, filling the whole drive behind her with light. But the car had started, picking up fast, without any lights on at all, until it had swung round the first corner. Then they came on again in full force, the first rush of speed slackened to the former steady pace of her drive from the station to Meadowside.

The driver, the same driver as before said, "You were punctual, miss. I was coming in to ask for you."

"Station, please," Judy said. She found she could not say more because her teeth were chattering and her head swimming and anyway, what the hell, it wasn't his business. She wondered if any of that evening had really been her own. But she remembered the look on Sir Edgar's face when the brandy so nearly hit it. That was enough. Never again. She should never have tangled with that man, nor Len, nor Chris. Chris. Poor Chris. Poor bloody drowned Chris.

She caught her train by the skin of her teeth, only because it was fifteen minutes late. She treated herself to another taxi from Waterloo back to Hampstead.

The car that had driven her to Meadowside and later back to Sunningdale station arrived at Scotland Yard at about the same time as Judy rang the bell at the Stockleys' house. The officer who had been such a help to her went in to make his report to Detective Superintendent Knox.

XIV

Detective Superintendent Knox was waiting patiently in his office at Scotland Yard, though midnight had passed and the report he had expected to get several hours ago had not yet arrived.

Ever since the inquest on Chris Trotter the detective superintendent, thoroughly dissatisfied with the verdict, had refused to give up his investigations into a death he had, from the time of the body's discovery, considered to be far from accidental. The inquest should have been adjourned after identification and medical evidence.

Police opinion was with him all the way. The boy had drowned when he was full of booze. Probably some brainless, wild party, somewhere along the Thames above the tide. His companions, also too drunk to save him, had then decided to save themselves trouble and blame by moving him down stream to where the tide and the river traffic would dispose of him. To conceal him if he should be picked up they had stripped him, perhaps tried to weight him in some way, though there was no direct evidence of this.

So the search up river began, very quietly, very thoroughly, for a house, and there were many, with lawns that reached the riverside and owners that entertained in a big way.

Until three weeks before the date of Sir Edgar's latest

party only five possible houses had been found that filled all the desired conditions. But only one of the owners had given a party and that had been an Edwardian-type garden party in the afternoon, with the local council and councillors and the local peasantry or its equivalent. Also a band. Not the sort of occasion young Trotter would have attended.

But then a report came to him from a detective sergeant who had taken his girl out in a punt while off-duty and had put in to the bank under some overhanging willows and had found the opening of a culvert at the river end. In the ordinary way he would not have paid any attention to it, his thoughts being elsewhere. But the girl had wanted to be put ashore where the bushes were thick and she had come back saying there was a swimming pool beyond the bank, with a sort of roof to it, but she hadn't dared look any further in case she was trespassing.

This was the first break in over a month, so Knox followed it up with hopeful energy. The pool was inspected quite openly through the local health authorities. Samples of the water were checked for bacterial content and an additional sample taken near the culvert was forwarded to the Yard, where it was shown to contain the same type of algae that had appeared in Chris Trotter's lungs and stomach.

Sir Edgar Seven had not been at home when the local officials called, but he had answered their notice requesting 'facilities for inspection' and they were not obstructed, but rather encouraged during their visit.

More followed. The Seven parties were held frequently. They were well attended, very noisy, notorious in the district. There had been no complaints in court, for no by-laws had been broken. But the nuisance value was high. Though the house was reasonably isolated, even at that fashionable point on the river's course, the approach to it was along several narrowing lanes leading from highways. So guests, often the worse for wear from too much entertainment of several kinds, sometimes got lost on their way home. When these parties broke up the lanes were filled with wavering headlights, loud cursing, shrill screams of abuse and even metallic raspings and bangs as the cars collided with walls, gate posts or one another. For these incidents the car owners could be brought to court or their insurers made to pay compensation. But Sir Edgar Seven himself had not offended, could not be faulted and would never say more than that young people did get wild these days and could afford it, unhappily!

Chris Trotter's death was perhaps a case in point, the detective superintendent thought. So he set himself to learn more about the work and activities of the firm of Solway, Seven, Export and Import consultants.

Nothing of any note came from a casual watch of arrivals and departures near the office block. Until a tip-off, that was as it turned out to be, a deliberate red herring, sent more plain-clothes men to that vicinity of the City in order to take them away from the area where a security van was to be held up and robbed. A young man noticed the Frobishers, saw them greet a smashing bird and the man go into the office block while the women went off together. By now the young detective had recognised the girl who had been on the front page of his daily paper and also on tele. He had dawdled over a cup of coffee at the next table to the two women and had heard, though imperfectly, some items of interest that connected the drowned C. Trotter with the owner of the riverside mansion near Sunningdale.

Detective Superintendent Knox pursued the connection further. It was not difficult to discover the dates on which extra local domestic staff was needed for parties at Meadowside. It was easy enough to watch arrivals for the parties, mostly by car, but sometimes by rail, when their host would send a car with a chauffeur to the station to pick up these visitors.

Judy's 'taxi' was one of Knox's roving officers, acting on his own initiative in the first place, but having reported his action, identifying his 'fare' with confidence. He was told to pick her up in two hours' time as she had requested.

The girl's obviously excited, slightly inebriated state seemed to the officer to need further attention. As soon as he had seen her board her train back to London he drove as quickly as he could back to Meadowside, leaving his car in a hedge nearby and mingling with the crowd of departing guests, where he picked up enough fragmented comment to put together an idea of what had happened at the pool. Then he drove to the yard, having radioed that he had something to report.

"She was definitely upset, sir," he told Knox. "Stood in the drive gasping. I backed off and opened the front passenger door for her and she jumped in before I had time to speak. Just said 'Station, please' and not another word till we got there."

"Had there been anything you saw or heard to upset her?"

"There was noise all the time from when I put her down at the door. Folk coming and after an hour or so going. More noise when I think they went down to the river, to that swimming pool. A real uproar just before this girl shot into the drive bang into my headlights."

"You were arriving to pick her up? Yes, we'd O.K.'d that."

"She'd asked me to. Two hours, she said. Said she could tell Sir Edgar she had ordered the taxi to come back for her. Save him offering to get his car out."

"H'm." Knox was impressed. "You'd almost think she was a bit wary of him, getting to Sunningdale so early. That would forestall him sending a car to meet her."

"It did, sir. Partly why I kept the time she gave me. And there was that extra shouting. I forgot to mention it when I radioed in thinking about that kid standing in the headlights, swaying about a bit, not scared, not really, but bloody wild."

"And this extra noise of shouting? What was it about?"

"From what I picked up, like I said, it was to the effect Sir Edgar had somehow had a ducking in the pool. I couldn't make out exactly how or why, but they seemed to think he had made an exhibition of himself, lost his temper entirely."

"Yes," said Detective Inspector Knox. "And you drove off quickly to avoid being noticed, so you didn't find out what had really happened?"

"No, sir."

"Never mind. You did very well. Get along home and have a go at finding it out tomorrow morning. You needn't start early. I'm sure Sir Edgar Seven keeps his evening parties out of the news media."

"Thank you, sir."

Sir Edgar's mishap at the swimming pool did not indeed find its way into any newspaper. But one of his secretaries at the office rang up Len's house to inquire after Miss Trebannon. Sir Edgar would like to have a word with her.

Clare, who answered the call, said Judy had come back quite safely the evening before. She had left for her home in Devon at nine that morning and had said she intended to write to Sir Edgar to thank him for a wonderful time and send her apologies for spilling her glass of brandy over his suit. She must have had rather too much to drink. Sir Edgar received this message from his secretary with apparently complete indifference.

Judy was happy to be back in Plymouth. She decided to forget the silly fuss over the book. She might not be going to get the fortune Len had promised her, but she had turned her prize into her marvellous little boat and that was more than she had ever expected to have so soon. Fantastic. Even

Dad said so. She had christened her pet *Adventurer*. Dad had insured the vessel with Lloyd's.

Mr. Smith had taken much more notice of his young daughter since she had taken him to see *Adventurer*. He judged rightly that she knew roughly how to manage the craft, for she had picked up a lot of useful skill going out with him to fish in his own old-fashioned drifter. But did she know enough about the engine? What would she do if it packed up at sea? He impressed upon her that she must either learn and practise more under tuition, preferably his, or else arrange always to have a man aboard who could do any tinkering that was needed.

"It's not as if you thought of taking her a real voyage," he explained as they idled gently on a mild November morning in Torbay. "You could be held up by a sudden blow any time off shore and need all your power to run home before it got too much."

"I could heave to, couldn't I?" she asked. "Like when we're fishing."

"May be. May be not. But the more you know and the more you get used to its whims, the safer you'll be if you haven't got me or some other bloke with you."

She did not tell him that she listened to all this chiefly because she had agreed to the Stockleys' plan. As soon as possible now, they would be off, making across the Channel to France. She had found a shop in Plymouth that sold charts and had, with a dinghy-sailing college aquaintance to help her understand them, succeeded in working out her route to the continent. Very sensibly she realised that the long trip round the Atlantic coast of France was outside her competence. Clare had said this too. It would have to be the canals, so she would cross to Cherbourg and move from there. She was entirely vague as to how she would get her boat into a suitable river or canal. She would keep on making inquiries until the Stockleys arrived. The sooner the better. It would be December before long. Short days.

143

Bad weather. Crazy perhaps, but that party had scared her.

No, the old goat had scared her. Because she wouldn't swim? Why so persistent? What had he got on Len, that he didn't want to back him any more? *What had he had on Chris? Drowned Chris?* And the instant diving bodyguard? *Why?*

She shivered as she followed the line of buoys back into Dartmouth harbour.

"Cold?" asked her father.

"Not really."

"You kids nowadays don't wear enough to be decent let alone warm. Get yourself a couple of sweaters and wear both."

"I'd be stifled. This jumper's enough."

"You'll be laying up for the winter soon, won't you? Better bring her round to Fred's wharf. He won't charge you more than he does me."

"I might do that," she said.

Judy was not alone in wondering about Sir Edgar's motives and actions. Detective Inspector Rickard had been to see the Frobishers again. He found them much more open now over their fostering of Chris Trotter. Aunt Muriel had confessed to her husband that her sense of outrage over the tycoon's ingratitude had led to her indiscreet disclosures to Judy Smith. So there was no point in concealing any longer the name of their sometime benefactor. Besides, all that pretence of accounts was over, the secrecy a myth. Sir Edgar was boss over the accountant; he was also of the lawyer; the boy was his sister's bastard and they now suspected the boy knew this, had known it for years.

"I wouldn't be surprised if he let his uncle know that he knew," Uncle Henry said.

Detective Inspector Rickard agreed and added, "Are you suggesting this had anything to do with his death?"

Aunt Muriel was shocked.

"You mean did Sir Edgar get rid of him?"

"If he was trying on blackmail? Chris, I mean?" Uncle Henry asked, nodding his head. "Well, I don't know that I'd put it past him."

"Well, no. I'm not suggesting anything," the detective inspector said, "I was asking if you were."

"Then I wasn't," Uncle Henry said firmly and left it at that.

But Rickard went away thinking that blackmail over a question of bastardy was hardly likely to succeed these days. No, if Chris was drowned to destroy his knowledge of some forbidden matter, then that secret must be far more deadly than a simple moral lapse on the part of the tycoon's sister. And what could that be and how could the young man have got hold of it?

Nevertheless it was very strange that young Trotter had died so conveniently, just as the unsuccessful publisher had at last made good by bringing out a book now reputed to have been stolen by the country girl who had been Trotter's bird, and moreover just when the plagiarism had been discovered. Detective Inspector Rickard reported his interview with the Frobishers to Detective Superintendent Knox. He also reported it to Detective Inspector Whimple at Feltbridge.

Whimple had followed the progress of the plagiarism as it had appeared in the local papers. Where there had been a sense of pride and achievement in the success of a local girl, and certainly a mad rush to get hold of *The Young Adventurers* either from the public libraries or in paperback, so now there was a move to protect her, to boost the theory that it was mere coincidence. They knew Judy had done some typing for the old authoress, so perhaps she had been influenced in the matter of the plot, but otherwise the two books were quite different.

The assistants in the public libraries said so. Disliking and envying Judy for her supposed talent, they were doing their best to push *The Eve of Yesterday*. They were having considerable success. The demand for the book induced them to buy several extra copies of it.

When Whimple paid a visit to Mrs. Grosshouse to discover how the case was being handled, he found her less angry than he had been led to expect.

"We would like to avoid a court case," Anita Armstrong told him. "Waste of money. There really is no defence."

He did not argue the point with her, but asked her if this meant some sort of agreed settlement. Would she be seeing Miss Trebannon about it?

"You mean Judy Smith? No, I won't be seeing her. God forbid! Lying little thief! Anyway, my publishers' lawyer and my agent's as well are dealing with her own phoney publisher."

Detective Inspector Whimple did not deny it, but said, "We are interested in your case, Mrs. Grosshouse, because both you and she live in our manor, or rather in our part of Devon. You have our telephone number at Feltbridge, I expect. May I give you my personal number in case you may have any cause to want to get in touch with me in a hurry?"

"Why should I?" she asked, slightly shaken. "What's in your mind?"

"Nothing definite. Nothing alarming, I assure you," he answered. "I just happen to know Miss—er—Smith is at present at Dartmouth living on a new cabin cruiser she has bought for herself."

"With my money!" Anita Armstrong said, hardly able to speak for the rage that suddenly gripped her at this news.

That evening the Hastons came over from Salcombe to dine at the cottage. Mrs. Droge had cooked the meal, but left as soon as the guests had swallowed their welcome drinks and were ready to eat. She had become somewhat dissatisfied with her position as housekeeper. When it involved looking after an elderly widow during her decline and perhaps profitably seeing her to the grave, she had been ready to extend herself. Now that the old lady had disclosed the meaning of her curious reticence in the past, capping it with notoriety, if not scandal, in the present and that on account of a piece of fiction, a type of reading Mrs. Droge never used and was inclined to disapprove of, she began to feel that a change might be desirable. Anyway someone so talented could look after her visitors without total paid help, no extra offered and none asked for. But lacking, all the same.

"What's got into Mrs. Droge?" Mervyn asked, as Mrs. Grosshouse collected the plates after the first course and went away to the kitchen.

"Crotchety. Often is," said Mrs. Grosshouse, returning with hot dishes on a tray.

"Let me help," Sarah offered. "I expect she feels you're getting too grand, Anita, with everyone talking about you and the book. Thinks she must take you down a peg or two."

"Nonsense. I'm sure she never thinks twice about the book. Or any book, for that matter."

"But it *is* doing very nicely, isn't it?" Mervyn insisted. "A just revenge. By her theft that girl has stirred the British non-reading public into mending its ways."

"I'm not sure I like the implications of that," Anita said, thoughtfully. But she smiled.

XV

Judy met the Stockleys at Kingswear and took them in her rubber dinghy to the smart little *Adventurer* moored opposite Dartmouth town. They each carried two large angular suitcases, which made two separate journeys necessary. Judy took Len and his cases over first, then went back for Clare, who seemed to be both bewildered and frightened.

"We can't cross the Channel in *this*!" she protested.

"Whyever not? Dad and I have had her out halfway there, fishing."

"Is he coming to drive it for us?"

Judy gave one of her coarse open-mouthed laughs at this land-lubber's talk.

"No. Certainly not. He and Ma don't even know I'm going. But I'll leave them a note. I won't let them think I've taken her out and drowned us all."

Clare shuddered, but she knew there was no future for Len and herself in England; not much hope anywhere else. Leave the country first and think again, later, she decided.

Judy explained her new plan. She agreed with Clare that the long voyage round the French and Spanish coasts to the Mediterranean was out. Far too late in the season. They would choose their weather for a quick dash across to Cherbourg or Le Havre and get into the river and canal network across France. It would be more exposed to official interruption and interference, but safer physically.

"Thank God for that," said Clare.

Len said nothing. At all costs he must avoid any discussion of the money angle until they had left England behind them. If possible. He dared not break the news of the collapse of his ailing business, his bankruptcy, Ned's total withdrawal of support. In fact his new demands for repayment of all the expenses connected with the pilfered book. Royalties due to Judy, up to the date of Haseldyne's action for plagiarism, had all gone to placating the more immediate and insistent of his creditors. In effect, though she did not know it yet, she had nothing coming to her and must be setting out with only the balance of her prize money, if indeed that too had not been recalled. All he could think of was their urgent need, all of them, to get away as quickly as possible.

"When do we start?" he asked, after Judy had shown him over the boat and he had admired the shining engines, the neat radio, the direction-finding apparatus and the echo-sounder for registering the depth of water beneath them.

He understood very little of these matters. It was Clare who said, "You must have charts, I suppose?"

"Of course I have. And a few books about France and the canals. I can't speak the lingo. Can either of you two?"

Unexpectedly Clare said she could manage a little, having been sent to a finishing school in Paris after she left her English establishment.

The weather forecast that evening was mixed, not very favourable. Judy found the shipping forecast, but that was even more daunting.

"We may have to put it off for a day or two," she told her friends.

"We can't," Len said, so firmly and despairingly that Judy began to be afraid. "Why not?" she demanded.

He drew a breath, began to speak, then jumped up and

went forward from the small enclosed wheelhouse to stand in the bows, staring down river to the bend that hid its progress to the sea.

It was late afternoon and the light was fading. In fact the town lights had been coming on for some time in a brilliant row along the quay and now up and down a high building. The College, on its hill, shone brightly, floodlit. Above Kingswear the lighthouse flashed its beam.

Judy went along the deck to join him. Without looking at her he said, "Apart from the weather is there any reason we can't get straight off now?"

"Yes, there is." She pointed at the water. "Tide's begun to come in. That's why we're facing down stream. I'm not going out till slack water. Then we'll have it with us to help clear the land. Clear the rocks near the mouth of the river." She grinned at him. "Dad's advice. I'm not an expert, you know."

"Then when can we go? What time?"

"About two or three in the morning."

"But it'll be dark."

"So it would be now. It doesn't matter. There are the lights, navigation lights, I mean. I've done it with Dad."

So they ate a meal out of tins and went to bed early. Judy set the alarm clock for three. She did not fancy going far in the dark after they left the mouth of the river because the fishing boats would be crowding in towards the entrance then, not expecting to meet summer craft like hers. She might find it tricky to make her way between them before the coming dawn began to light up their hulls and connect these with their masthead and side lights.

At three the river was smothered by a thick sea mist, even the town quay and dinghy basin hidden. The three frustrated travellers had a silent breakfast together.

At five the mist was thinning and a wind from the southeast, that came to them where they lay as a strong breeze up river, was blowing in past them in swirling clouds.

"We can't possibly sail in a fog," Clare protested. All night she had tried to think of some other way, some less terrifying means, of leaving the country.

Judy, who had listened to the shipping forecast, said, "It will be gone soon now. It's the wind is the real problem. Ought to be in the west this time of year but they say it's south-east, fresh."

"What does that mean?"

"More than I'd bargained for. We have to go though, Len says."

"We have to go," he insisted. "It's that or—"

"Or what?" Clare's voice had risen towards hysteria.

"Shut up!" Judy told her roughly. "Come on, Len, help me get the engine warmed up."

They got everything put away and fastened down, as Judy had been brought up to do. Len dropped the mooring buoy overboard as Judy began to creep forward and they were off, gliding smoothly, and quite fast, on the ebbing tide, now nearing slack water.

Judy knew the way out of the river, she had no trouble finding the course to the open sea, but her companions, who had enjoyed the feeling of escape and the pleasant movement in the river, began to lose confidence as the swell increased and the waves, small at first, but soon white-tipped, slapped and sucked and slapped again.

Their course was set for the Channel Islands; their nearest goal, almost due south. Those other ports further east lay dead to windward. They could not possibly reach them, Judy decided, bracing herself at the wheel as the waves grew, mounting against the current, thumping *Adventurer*, pouring green over her dipping bows, shaking her, plunging her until her big screw bit on spray, only for a moment, so that she lost momentum and at the next instant was driving her forward through deep water at her stern, into the next big on-coming roller.

In twenty minutes Len was stumbling below, vomiting as

151

he went. Clare crouched on the deck of the wheelhouse, green-faced, speechless, too collapsed to attempt the companionway. She longed for the warmth of the cabin and for a bunk on which to lay her throbbing head, but it was impossible without Judy's help and the girl could not leave her post.

Judy held her course defiantly, until a horrid thought came to her. Looking back she saw they were at most some three miles from the mouth of the Dart. They were clear of all the rocks within a mile of it, but they were not heading for the Channel Islands, they were sliding in a westerly drift, driven by that fresh wind from the south-east that was already freshening still more, for 'fresh' in shipping parlance means a gale to yachtsmen.

What should she do? Push on south-west, which might mean progress but to what possible port? Dad had warned her several times against the north coast of Brittany. Rocks for five miles off shore and a low coast line. Well buoyed and with beacons and lighthouses to mark the intricate ways into the rivers and ports. But she would never find them. Besides, she had not enough fuel in her comparatively small tank to take her all the extra distance.

She lashed the wheel and left it, first to dispose of Clare below, who sank, unprotesting, speechless, on to the empty bunk. Len raised a white face, but gave one groan and lay back. Useless, both of them, Judy realised.

She consulted the petrol gauge and went back to the wheel. Now there was only one decision to make. Back to Dartmouth, which would be comparatively easy, though it meant more battling against the wind, or more easily, though much further, on to Plymouth.

Well, why not Plymouth? Dad was there and home. In her present discomfort and the unexpected defeat of her plans she longed, little-girl like, for immediate rescue, not from the boat or the sea, but from a new, very unpleasant sense of her own limitations. But she did have an instinctive respect for the immense power of sea and wind, for she had been brought up with them beside her, so she looked at the chart she had pinned up to guide the start of her voyage and stared at the coast line of England, still not further off than some five miles.

Start Point lay ahead to starboard of her bows; all beyond was mist and spray, but she did not expect to see land for she knew that it fell away in a wide long sweep until it dipped again south to the Lizard. She must fight her way out from this lee shore to get clear of the Start, then she could turn off this bloody wind and make for Plymouth Sound. In any case she could point her way south-west now and to hell with France.

But the wind continued to freshen and the waves attacking her now on the quarter drenched the deck and invaded the puny shelter where she stood. She dared not open the throttle, she knew that Dad would by now have hove to. Or would he, with the menace of Start Point, still there, not yet safely on her beam. And the petrol too. She must crawl along to preserve that until they could get this easterly blow well behind them.

When the Start did fall back and ahead she could see Prawle Point with beyond it Bolt Head, she did alter course a little to starboard to make the movement easier. With the wind and waves more directly behind her, she lashed her helm again and took a very rapid look below.

She must tell her passengers, she could not call them crew, what she had decided to do. After she had checked the petrol gauge this was worse than she had hoped. There was enough to make Salcombe but not Plymouth.

Len, still utterly prostrate, only groaned. Clare was roused to protest. She was furious.

"You devil!" she screamed. "You never meant to take us to France. You put us through this ghastly, this—" She gulped for words to describe her sufferings, but not finding them whispered, "We could have gone by air."

"And been stopped at the airport," Judy said, scornfully. "Don't tell me Len has clothes in that second suitcase. Nor have you got cosmetics in your second bag. His is the book and yours his dope. Right?"

She got no answer so she turned away to the hatch and climbed back to the bridge and the wheel.

Though the wind was almost dead behind them now she found *Adventurer* had drifted in towards the land beyond Prawle Point and was now not more than a couple of miles off, if as much. Bolt Head reared up to port, much further away. She took a quick look at the chart, remembering suddenly some of Dad's objections to Salcombe as a harbour. The bar, of course, the bar of sand, with a channel away over to the left and then navigation posts and lights to keep in line as you entered or left.

She swung the wheel, leaning to take the expected dip and swoop. So the knife in Clare's hand plunged into the chart, not into Judy's back and Clare's body, off balance, fell against her, heavy, clumsy, too shocked by her failure to take fresh action

But not for long. As Judy flung her off and *Adventurer*, out of control, began to broach to, taking the big wave broadside across the deck, the two women struggled fiercely for possession of the knife. Clare grasped the handle and pulled it free, Judy brought the edge of her hand down on the other's wrist in a karate chop. It should have broken the bones, but the violent movement of the boat took away too much of the force behind it and Clare simply dropped the weapon, which skittered about the deck, Judy diving after it, Clare, mad with fury, flinging herself at the enemy she had hated and feared from the first moment they had met.

The end of the fight came quickly. Clare had hold of Judy's duffle coat; she tore it away as the girl pulled her arms free. They were stumbling and wrestling in the wheelhouse opening when Judy saw the knife at her feet. She

154

stooped for it, Clare pushed at her with frantic power, Judy stumbled out below the guard rail along the length of the vessel, Clare flung herself at her again and Judy was overboard, the sea curling and foaming to take her.

Instinctively she took it in a dive, shocked by the cold that struck to the core of her body, but relieved to be parted from the maniac aboard.

She came up to find there were already several yards between them. There was no sign of Clare; but obviously there was no possible way of getting back on board and she did not expect to have much time before her. How lucky that Clare had pulled off her duffle coat. With its weight about her arms and chest she would have no chance at all. Without it her jeans did not matter and she managed to drag off her yachting plimsolls before she settled to the long swim for the shore.

Lucky again, she decided, for the fight had put them back towards the starboard side of the harbour mouth where there were sandy beaches if only she could reach them. She determined to reach them.

There were moments when she became so tired that the effort did not seem worth maintaining, when it would have been easy to let go. The cold that by now had made her hands and feet numb, unfeeling, did not bother her chest any longer. The dreaded cramp was still a threat. If only she had been able to get some lunch. It must be well on into the afternoon now. The sea was getting smoother, near the end of the ebb again and at last in the lee of Prawle Point.

When her feet touched bottom Judy stood up, but fell down again at once, swallowed sea water and swore obscenely. She swam on, with a stony uninviting shore ahead, then stood up again, looking back towards Bolt Head. She saw her poor little *Adventurer*, still broached to, rolled and smothered in breaking waves suddenly up-end, swing round, and crash back again as the bar took her. In another instant she had disappeared.

Cursing, crying, calling aloud for revenge, for help to take revenge, Judy stumbled up the beach. There was no one there. Scrub land with beyond fields and cattle grazing. No house, cottage or barn. No human beings.

She staggered on to find shelter and food. The hard earth, stones, sand, prickly sea plants, coarse grass, beat her naked feet into active circulation, though her hands and arms were as numb as before. Presently she knew she could not go on. She found shelter in the hedge above a narrow lane. She was asleep as soon as her head touched the rounded edge of a narrow ditch.

It was Sarah Haston who noticed the little white cabin cruiser behaving strangely just off the harbour entrance.

"Vyn!" she called. "There's another mug asking for trouble at sea. Bring the glasses. It looks serious."

"It *is* serious," he answered, focussing on the boat. "With the sea that's running they won't get over the bar. Better get on to the coastguards." .

"This is the fourth time this season."

"The season was over six weeks ago. This is a set of madmen, but—"

"Or mad women—"

"But I can't see any sign of life on deck. Yes, I can. Something stirring in the wheelhouse. Hurry up with the call, Sally."

The call was heeded, for the Hastons, who had acted during the last two years as extra voluntary look-outs, were fully respected for the worthwhile calls they made.

It was not more than twenty minutes before local help from Salcombe was on the scene. But the cabin cruiser had struck the bar, capsized and sunk before help arrived, so a search began for possible survivors. This went on for several hours, during which Clare Stockley, drowned and dead, was washed into their sight by the now flooding tide. They picked her up and took her back to Salcombe and

156

from there transported her to Feltbridge where the police took charge of her.

Any other people on the cabin cruiser must have been trapped and drowned on the bar. The vessel would be raised and searched the next day when its identity and that of its owner, knowledge of where it had come from, where it intended to go and everything else about it would be made plain. The rescuers had the impression that Detective Inspector Whimple, who spoke to them after directing the recovered body to the mortuary, did already know the answers to some of these questions. But they did not report this to the Hastons when they rang up Mervyn to tell him of the single depressing result of their efforts.

About six hours later there was an explosion in the entrance to Salcombe Harbour. It was not very loud, a dull, thudding explosion from the spot on the bar where *Adventurer* had sunk. A spurt of water shot up into the surrounding darkness; later a few ragged pieces of wood floated away, but not many and there was no further disturbance.

Mrs. Grosshouse was sipping her nightly mug of chocolate when her house bell rang feebly, reinforced by a loud bang from her door knocker.

"Damn," she said aloud, but she went to the door and opened it.

A wretched bedraggled figure stood there, wet clothes clinging to a girl's figure, hair plastered darkly to a small round head, bare muddy feet streaked with blood, red scratches on hands and arms. Alarming, pitiable, but easily recognised.

"Judy!" said Mrs. Grosshouse. "The thieving bitch herself!"

"Help me!" the girl pleaded in a hoarse whisper. "Please help me. *Please!*" She swayed and fell forward on her knees.

"Oh hell's bells and bloody brimstone!" roared Mrs. Grosshouse, reverting to a very distant past and a younger brother's schoolboy curse.

Judy giggled. Mrs. Grosshouse pulled her forward over the threshold and banged the door shut behind her. She heaved her unwanted, hated visitor to her feet, helped her into the sitting room, pushed her into an armchair and thrust her scarcely begun mug of hot chocolate into the grimy shaking hands.

"Drink that," she said. "I'll go and make some more."

She did so. She made two more mugs full, one for herself and another one for Judy. Into the girl's mug she poured a good spoonful of rum and a little of the same into her own. She collected a patterned tin of biscuits and returned with the lot on a tray to the sitting room.

The girl had drained the first mug; she had pulled up her chair very close to the fire in the cottage hearth; her clothes were steaming; her hands and feet had lost their blue-grey colour.

"You look as if you've come up from the bottom of the sea," Mrs. Grosshouse told her.

"It was an eff—, bloody long swim," Judy said.

Mrs. Grosshouse nodded.

"I can believe it," she said. "Drink this. Have some biscuits. Don't talk till you've finished. Then tell me—truthfully if you can—what has happened."

XVI

Judy's explanation, which did not come at once, was built on the model she had used for Ned. It did not come at once, because the rum in her cocoa, added to the warmth of the fire and the drying of her body, had restored her bruised courage and her undestroyed optimism to the point of further demand.

"That was fantastic," she said, holding out her empty mug to Mrs. Grosshouse. "I haven't had a thing all day. You wouldn't have a bit of pie or a sausage roll or something by any chance, would you? I'm literally starving."

"I'll see," her rescuer answered. "Mrs. Droge manages my larder, but I expect I can find something. I usually make myself an omelette for supper. Mrs. Droge did bring me in some free range eggs today."

"She still working here?" Judy asked as Mrs. Grosshouse moved away to the door.

"She still looks after me, bless her."

Before the old bag came back with the eats and please God not a grotty omelette, Judy thought, she must get her story sorted out a bit. Put it all on Len, as before, but bring in Ned, call him Sir Edgar Seven though, very keen to fight the case. Why? Ask another. To herself, all along, she had asked this question and failed to answer it.

Mrs. Grosshouse put together a sustaining meal made up of half a small pork pie, a thick slice of brown bread, a hunk of local cheese, butter, home-grown lettuce and tomatoes. For pudding a small round strawberry tart with a spoonful of clotted cream on top.

Judy sighed with pleasure when she saw this feast and did not speak until the plates were empty.

"Now then," said Mrs. Grosshouse. "I want to know your story, the real truth, mind. Why you have come to me, straight out of the sea, apparently. Have you wrecked your little luxury launch? And who else, I wonder? Go ahead. Out with it."

She did not tell the girl that before getting together the food for her meal she had crept upstairs to her bedroom and on the telephone extension, with her head and the machine covered by her eiderdown, she had rung up the Hastons to declare her news of the unwelcome visitor and her growing fear of the girl. They promised to come to her at once. It was too late for the ferry; it would have to be the long way round. So Judy's tale must take some time to tell. She must help with questions to open it out.

Judy worked slowly, carefully, to establish her own outraged innocence in the matter of plagiarism. At this stage of the wrong-doing, Chris Trotter had been the chief villain, but Len Stockley had confused her, pretending that he would publish for Mrs. Grosshouse right up until she went off to Italy without a word over the end of the novel.

"Never occurred to me," Mrs. Grosshouse interrupted, adding with a short laugh, "didn't know myself at that point."

"It was when you didn't answer my letter. Len, I mean Mr. Stockley, began to write the last part himself. And I was to do the talking bits."

"You mean the dialogue?"

"That's right. So then I did it through right from the beginning to make it match up. So in a way, Mrs. Grosshouse, it really *was* my book that got the prize."

"You damned, deceitful, lying little thief!" Anita Armstrong burst out. "I ought to—" She broke off, staring at the girl, who looked steadily back at her, hard eyes glinting in the beautiful face where the streaks of sea water had dried in a pale crust of salt like misapplied face powder.

Judy went on with her tale. Len's wife Clare misunderstood her connection with Len. She was jealous for no reason, especially after Chris was drowned. Before that she'd understood that Chris was her, Judy's boy friend. A little digression about the Frobishers seemed useful here, with a garbled account of the foster parents and of Chris's drinking habits, but nothing about his connection with Ned.

"My publisher is taking the case, not me," Mrs. Armstrong said. "They are insured against this type of theft as against libels and so on."

Judy thought it would be as well to go on about the voyage and its end.

"Clare went for me in the wheelhouse," she said. "It was bad enough trying to get to the harbour entrance from the Start."

"You mean Start Point?"

"Of course. We were too near Prawle, I knew, but I could have made it if she hadn't come up with a knife. She was mad, stark staring bonkers."

"You went overboard to avoid her?"

"We were fighting. I slipped and she pushed."

"So you swam away and left them to their fate."

"I couldn't have got back, could I? That sea and the engine still on, Clare below again I expect, no rope to get hold of or anything? I ask you!"

"So you swam. How far?"

"How do I know? Miles, it felt like in the end. Don't ask me. I thought I'd had it."

She seemed genuinely moved at last. She put her hands, dirty, blood-streaked, to her face, shuddered again and crouched lower in her chair.

The swim was true, at least, Mrs. Grosshouse decided,

however much the early part of the tale was not. Probably this stupid, greedy, but brave and determined girl was telling most of what she thought was the truth. A point struck her.

"Why did you come to me, of all people?" she asked.

Judy sat up. Did the old harridan imagine she came to her on purpose.

"I didn't know it would be you till you opened the door," she said. "I passed out when I got ashore. I don't know how long. Still light then, just. Hadn't got the time. Watch drowned, of course. This was the first house where I saw a light, so I knocked. It had to be you. Oh God, I do feel awful!"

"Probably eaten too much, too soon," was the unsympathetic response.

"Big help, aren't you?"

Mrs. Grosshouse, whose temper was rising, whose patience, born of pity, had come to its meagre end, found herself longing to be rid of this unwanted fugitive, but uncertain how to manage it. Judy, unless she was going to be sick, was so much stronger than herself that she dared not try.

A combined knock and ring at the front door brought her instant relief. She hurried out. Behind her she heard Judy give a strangled scream.

"Sarah! Mervyn! Thank God! She's still here. Come in and tell me what to do with her."

A third figure appeared from behind the Hastons. Mervyn said, "We told your news to Feltbridge. Inspector Whimple was available so we brought him along."

Detective Inspector Whimple gave a hand to Mrs. Grosshouse, then slipping past the three of them went quickly into the sitting room, saying as he did so, "Good evening, Miss Smith. I congratulate you on your escape from a sinking ship. I'd like to know how you managed it."

Judy had scrambled to her feet when she heard voices,

one of which she recognised, in the hall. She turned to Mrs. Grosshouse who had hurried to her side, said in a fierce whisper, "Bloody grass!" and spat straight into her face.

There was instant protest. Sarah raised a hand to smack the dreadful girl's face, Mervyn prevented this action, Mrs. Grosshouse burst into tears, her friends led her away to the bathroom to clean her outraged features.

Detective Inspector Whimple said, "You shouldn't have done that, Miss Smith. Mrs. Grosshouse informed the Hastons you had come to her for help. It was Mr. Haston rang Feltbridge."

Judy was silent, unrepentant, her slow mind fully alert, searching for a reason why the Law, the pigs as Chris always called them, should want to see her. The answer was very simple.

"So we were able to notify your father of your escape," Whimple went on. "Relieve his mind and your mother, too. They had been informed of the wreck earlier."

"How?" she asked, stung by surprise out of her surliness and frantic inner questioning.

"By the rescue launch. You were not found so he was told you were missing. When we rang him you had turned up he said he'd fetch you home from Feltbridge. He'll be on his way now. Mr. Haston will drive us back there, now."

"No!" she said loudly.

"Yes," said Mervyn, coming back into the room with a rug over his arm. "Don't be tiresome, Judy. Say thank you to Mrs. Grosshouse who is longing to see the last of you."

He flung the rug over her shoulders and with it pinning her arms forced her defeat without a struggle.

"Slippers," said Sarah, putting down an old pair on the floor. Judy kicked them away.

"O.K. No slippers," said Whimple, adding his practised weight to the ejection. "The back seat, sir, please, and Mrs. Haston on the other side of her from me."

In this fashion with Judy again silent, but unresisting, they settled their captive into the car and Mervyn drove away.

Mrs. Grosshouse poured herself a restoring drink, brandy this time. Then she went to bed.

At Feltbridge police station Judy was put in a small bare room, still wrapped in the rug and left there. After a few minutes a uniformed police woman came in to ask her if she needed the toilet. As she did and fairly urgently, she was led to a lavatory and later having given herself an extensive, much needed wash, was led back. Detective Inspector Whimple joined them and sat down at the central table, opposite Judy. The police woman stood behind her, the detective prepared to take notes.

Judy said, "You told me Dad was coming to take me home."

"So he is," Whimple answered. "He must be on his way."

"Taking his time, isn't he?"

"Not really. I couldn't tell him before we got here. I didn't know definitely it was really you until I saw you in Siddicombe."

The logic of this escaped her; the fuzz was only proving its usual awfulness.

"Of course you knew. Why would old Mrs. Grosshouse make a mistake. I was soaked, done in—"

"You might have been Mrs. Stockley. Dartmouth knew you had two others on your boat."

"How?" Judy was astonished. She had imagined her presence on board, the departure as the early mist cleared, had all gone unremarked.

"Well, you didn't pay your harbour dues before leaving, did you? The harbour master notified this. He knew your father. Didn't you ever meet him? Didn't you ever know the rules? He knew you'd left all right. And as you didn't tell him your destination either, he gathered you were not going overseas."

"I was taking my boat to Plymouth," Judy said, knowing the lie could never be proved now.

"And the weather and your inexperience got the better of you. But why try for Salcombe? Didn't you know the bar is at its most dangerous at low water when there are steep waves?"

"I was afraid I'd not have enough petrol to make Plymouth."

"Because you'd started for France and got nowhere?"

"Because I had to get out far enough to make Start Point."

They stared at one another. Whimple tried again.

"Tell me why you abandoned ship when you knew your passengers were incapable of managing your boat?"

"I never!" Judy, highly indignant, told him the unlikely, but true story of her fight to ward off Clare, how she was forced to her knees and pushed overboard.

Again Whimple gave up an argument neither could win. Shock tactics, he decided, might break this stubborn witness.

He allowed a significant pause, during which he inquired outside whether Mr. Smith had arrived to fetch his daughter and found that he had not.

He sat down again, made a note of the time and said, "Now tell me about your visit to Sir Edgar Seven's house by the Thames on—" He paused to consult his file, "On November 10th?"

Judy gasped. This was appalling. How on earth?—

"I never—" she began automatically, but he checked her with an impatient gesture. "Don't be stupid. You were a close friend of Chris Trotter and he was closely connected with Sir Edgar and with the Frobishers at Minehead. They have given valuable information that I think you shared. We know you were invited to one of his notorious parties.

You left it rather suddenly. I should like you to tell me about the party."

Judy understood at last. No magic, just that rotten taxi driver, self-hire my foot, another of the pigs, sent to spy on her. Why! *Why!* All the same he had been damned useful. She remembered her unreasoning fear, her spontaneous response to old Ned's badgering, his skidding feet, his almighty splash, the three lithe forms of his bodyguards diving, her mad flight—

"I left because I was bored," she managed to say, still reliving the awfulness of that encounter. "I didn't want to swim. He tried to make me. He fell in the pool. I left, I daren't stay. It was so awful. All those posh types, staring, insulting. I just wanted out. If your sneaking pig hadn't been there—"

"You thought you might turn up like Chris, or even never turn up, didn't you? *Didn't you!*" Whimple shouted.

Judy collapsed in tears at last. The police woman looked furious, but produced a handkerchief. Detective Inspector Whimple, a trifle ashamed, but satisfied with this wholly negative evidence, closed his file and went away.

Half an hour later Judy's Dad arrived, bringing various articles of clothing, including socks and shoes, recommended by Feltbridge police and put together by Judy's mother.

Mr. Smith was still fuming over the loss of his daughter's lovely little cruiser in which he had looked forward to much fishing and cruising during the next season. But when he saw her and understood the trial and terror she had surmounted he was more inclined to make excuses for her reckless misjudgment of the weather and the time of year and above all her failure to notify him of her intention to take her boat out to sea without him on board.

"Always a self-willed one," he told Detective Inspector Whimple. "Lucky to get away with it."

"The other two didn't," Whimple told him. "One stiff

picked up. The other's still in the cabin, we reckon. They'll lift the craft out when the weather slackens. Tomorrow or the day after. I'd keep her in bed with a sedative for a time if I were you. Get a doctor to her. Late shock pretty sure, I'd say."

Mr. Smith agreed, though he did not think this programme would work. In which he was quite correct. Judy slept all the way home in the car and for twelve hours thereafter. But she woke to demand a large meal and then went out to find some of her friends and excite them with a very garbled account of her adventure.

XVII

For another twenty-four hours the easterly wind blew and the wild white horses leaped and broke over the bar at Salcombe harbour. But on the second morning a vessel arrived from Plymouth with lifting gear and anchored in the dredged channel close to Bolt Head. She had a diver on board whose job it was to locate the cabin cruiser, establish whether the body of Leonard Stockley was on board and advise how best the small craft could be raised to the deck of the work ship or alternatively lifted to the surface, pumped out and perhaps towed into Salcombe for necessary repairs.

The diver found the sunken craft lying on its side, the battered wheelhouse and bridge up against the sand bar, a gaping hole in the bottom on the seaward side. There was no access to the cabin except by this hole, and it was not large enough to admit the diver and was besides stopped up by a large object, probably a suitcase, he reported.

In the end they managed to fix a wide sling over the hole and with ropes fore and aft drag the cruiser clear, lift her enough to make the sling taut and finally to deliver her on the deck of the salvage vessel.

The door of the hatch from the wheelhouse was jammed by broken parts of that crushed section of the wreck. It was not difficult to clear away; fortunately it had prevented the cabin from being scoured by the sea, otherwise than by the hole in the bottom. This had blasted away the bilges and part of the cabin sole, but had not allowed the larger contents to escape. The object the diver had seen blocking the hole was indeed a suitcase. There was another above it and on top of that the body of a man, presumably that of the missing member of the party, the publisher, Leonard Stockley.

As soon as these discoveries had been noted the salvage captain, who had merely looked down from above before pushing the hatch door into place again, gave orders to make the wreck fast where she was on his deck and fix tarpaulins over her. He then weighed anchor and set off back to Plymouth.

The diver, warming up after his chilly, but fairly short spell on the sea bed, stood beside the salvage captain, thinking over what he had seen.

"That hole," he remarked presently. "How did that come, I wonder?"

The captain, who had not bothered to look at it said, "Potty little eggshells, these fancy pleasure boats. Not built for real off-shore work. Match sticks."

"It was on the wrong side," the diver said.

"Of the boat? The seas came in that side, didn't they? Smashing against it. Weak spot in a plank, I suppose."

"No. I mean the wrong side of the hull. It wasn't the breaking in from the outside. It was something from inside, breaking outwards. As if—"

He stopped suddenly.

"Well, as if what?"

"An explosion of some sort," said the diver.

The captain laughed.

"With all that water about I don't see how the galley could go up. Or the petrol tank either."

"Something did," said the diver. "The wood round the edges is frayed outwards. You should take a look at it."

The captain did so, with the result that he got in touch at

169

once with his boss at the salvage company's headquarters in Plymouth and was told to get back at once and in the meantime do nothing further in the detective line. In fact he was not to touch the wreck. Others would be ready waiting at his home wharf to take over full responsibility.

The others proved to be the head of the firm with several members of the police, including Detective Inspector Whimple, escorting a white-faced Judy Smith, with her mother to support her, ready but shrinking from her duty to identify the dead man in the cabin. An ambulance was also at hand on the quayside and it was the ambulance men who brought the dead man ashore on a stretcher, after the body had been retrieved from among the other piled, broken rubbish in the cabin. They took the stretcher into the ambulance, where they cleared the sea-wrack and sand from the dead face and covered the rest of the form up to the chin.

So Judy found her unpleasant task in no way terrifying. The interior of the ambulance was just like a little hospital, she told her mother afterwards. It had a strongly antiseptic smell and poor old Len's face, in spite of being a nasty grey-mauve colour, was easily recognisable.

They did not tell her that most of the back of his head was missing; she did ask why his head was closely bandaged all over, but the answer that it was routine satisfied her, seemingly. Her ordeal lasted no more than five minutes and after she had signed the necessary statement of recognition, she was led away from the ambulance to a waiting car that took her and her mother home. But not before she had asked Detective Inspector Whimple how soon the cruiser would be released to be handed over to a shipyard for repairs.

"My dad said to ask you," she explained. "He had it insured for me. He said they'd need to look at the damage before they'd pay up."

"Did he?" Whimple said. "Well, tell him I suggest you notify your insurance—"

"I did that yesterday," she interrupted. "I want to know when I can tell them to see it."

Cold-hearted little bitch, Whimple thought, didn't turn a hair back there in the ambulance and not a murmur of grief, not even pity, for those two companions, both dead, while she swam ashore and walked four miles to Siddicombe to get help from the old lady she had cheated and robbed. Cold-hearted, tough with it, but ignorant too. She wasn't the only one; a pretty usual type of young delinquent, only more determined than most.

"We shall want a full statement of your trip round from Dartmouth, Miss Smith," he said, speaking through the open back window of the car that was to take her home. "Better be after we've sorted out the contents of the cruiser and listed them. You'll be able to claim your own property and we shall dispose of the Stockleys' things to any relatives they have when we have contacted them. I think you said you didn't know of any, except some casual mention of an aunt in France."

"Friend of an aunt in France. I never knew the name or the address."

"Well, think it over, you might remember. But you can expect me at your place, Mrs. Smith," he added, speaking directly to the girl's mother.

"Better ring up or we might be out," Mrs. Smith said, ungraciously. She was cold and bored and resented this dragging out of the proceedings.

"I'll do that."

He turned away, Judy wound up the window, the driver said, "O.K. then?" without turning his head and the car moved off.

On board the salvage vessel the police had cleared all movable objects throughout the cruiser and laid them out on deck on a wide canvas sheet. A great many fittings and household goods had been destroyed, a few, washed about and up and down had survived. After the cruiser sank on the seaward side of the bar she had lain below wave level at all but low water on the ebb, so the initial bashing had not been repeated. Drawers and cupboards that had remained shut disclosed their contents, wet but otherwise whole. This applied to clothes and a good many food tins, though cartons and packets were ruined. The women's handbags were found intact, also Len's wallet, that he had stowed in a small cupboard beside his bunk. There were three passports, travellers' cheques and currency, French and English, all sodden, all placed carefully in polythene for inspection after drying out.

But a more important find and one that most interested both the police, the salvage crew and the assessor of the marine insurance company was discovered in the bilges below the cabin sole. It became plain as soon as they had removed all the loose objects, including the four large, dented, but otherwise intact suitcases, two plain, the other two marked with the initials L.A.S., supposedly those of Leonard Stockley. For about midships there was a hole, where the floorboards had been forced up, torn, splintered, as from a blow. A blow dealt from below and matching in size and position the hole already noted in the cruiser's bottom, a little to one side of the keel, where the outer planks of the hull had been torn and forced in the opposite direction.

"An explosion!" several voices cried as the matter explained itself. And others cried, "How?"

They examined the engine, which had survived until waterlogged and seemed to be still firm and undamaged in its carefully constructed bed. The petrol tank and its connections were also intact, though the tank was empty.

"The girl said she'd been afraid she was running out of juice," Whimple said. "There doesn't seem to be any loose petrol around in the cabin, but would it have been washed out?"

"Probably." The assessor was hunting about in the

bilges. "But I rather think—" He was getting together a few scraps of metal and wire. "Most of the useful—" He went on searching then scrambled up, to sit on the dented edge of the bunk, staring down at the hole.

"I should say at this stage, in this position, away from any fire-producing system whatever, the explosion was man-made, deliberate, not accidental."

"And that," Whimple answered on an indrawn breath, "calls for a very full investigation."

"I thought you said there is only one survivor?"

"That's right. But not the kind to think up blowing a hole in her own boat, not even to get rid of two serious obstacles in her path."

"I don't get you," the assessor said, who had not heard the full story of the wreck nor seen the sole survivor.

"Not with herself on board, she wouldn't," Whimple added. "Some sort of bomb?" he asked gravely. "Time bomb, I suppose?"

"Why do you suppose that?"

"Well, if it was it must have been put on board in a harbour and that would be Dartmouth where it's been since she bought it. And not timed to go off there, calling attention to the accident, would it?"

"Down there in the bilges around midships, the sort of size it must have been, it was probably meant to blow a hole in the bottom and sink her. So presumably it was to happen at sea. Disappearance with all hands, that sort of thing."

Detective Inspector Whimple straightened up as well as he could, for his head just touched the cabin roof.

"Confirm that if you can," he said, "and let us have your report. I'll leave you to it."

He went away to help with the removal of the sad jumble lying on the canvas sheet. He took the four limp battered smelly suitcases to the boot of his own car and forced them open in his own office. Two held clothes, one a man's and one a woman's. In each of the other two lay a sodden mass

173

of paperbacks, stuck together, disintegrating, but all, apparently, of the same title and production, *The Young Adventurers*.

Whimple's interview with Judy took place the next morning, after he had received a further verbal report from the insurance assessor.

"I found several more bits of positive evidence of a small, low-powered bomb," the man said. "They will need further analysis. Also on the torn wood some fragments I strongly suspect belong to the brains and skull of the stiff whose head was bashed in. Must have been lying on the floorboards just above the thing when it went off. I'll confirm later."

Whimple did not give Judy all these details. In fact he began by taking a recording of her adventure from start to finish.

"It's very deceptive lying up at Dartmouth," the girl explained. "I knew not to go out until the fog lifted, but the tide was right, I daren't miss it, and you don't feel the wind, not rightly, till you get outside."

"Depends on the direction it comes from." said Whimple, who also fished in the sea at weekends off duty. "You didn't think to ask advice from your dad?"

"I didn't want him to know we intended to leave the country."

She made this disclosure in her usual voice, with a blank expression on her lovely face and in her big eyes, an expression the detective knew well in his wide experience of lawbreakers. It might be true, it might be a lie. You never knew which with the born criminal. In this case he believed her, on account of the bomb. He began to make calculations.

"Give me the times again. When you left harbour, how long you held your course. For the Channel Islands, was it?"

"When I found I couldn't possibly lay Cherbourg or Havre. Even so I was being blown down Channel."

"On a lee shore," said Whimple, nodding confirmation.

"Yes. So I altered to Plymouth. Not much better, you know, as I had to pass the Start."

Again Whimple nodded. Then, slowly and clearly he explained what would have happened to her cruiser in mid-Channel if she had held her original course. That really shook her.

"The bloody bastard!" she whispered, her face gone white and strained.

"Who?"

He was quick, but Judy was even quicker. In a slightly rougher voice than before she exclaimed against vandals, hooligans, muggers, envy and spite because she'd been lucky and won herself a fortune and got herself a boat for her own and her dad's pleasure.

He did not believe a word of it, but he knew he had lost his chance. Only that she must have a real enemy, and as she had shown worry, if not fear, when the Yard man had picked her up after her party at Meadowside and her encounter with Sir Edgar Seven, he must surely be that enemy.

He decided to drop this conclusion as far as the girl was concerned, but it was something that would be of great interest to Detective Superintendent Knox in connection with young Chris Trotter, drowned in fresh water, late nephew, according to the Frobishers, of this same Sir Edgar Seven.

"Where did you aim to end up in France?" he asked, hoping an abrupt change of direction might shake the girl again, and more profitably.

"The Mediterranean," she answered at once. "By canal or river."

"You had charts?"

"Maps."

"Currency?"

"What's that?"

"Money. Currency is cash. Or travellers' cheques."

"Both."

"Enough?"

"How do I know?" Seeing the disbelief in his face she added, "Len said he had a reserve but he didn't say where."

Whimple said slowly, "I think I can tell you where. Two of his suitcases were full of mashed up sodden paperback copies of that book he brought out as written by you."

"*The Young Adventurers*?" Judy's eyes sparkled. She gave one of her loud laughs, all her strong white teeth showing as she threw back her head. "Just like—" She gulped, went on soberly, "He'd hoped to sell them abroad for dough. It was doing very well up to this fuss over the old harridan's novel."

It was an explanation. Judy seemed to think it authentic. He found he had no more questions to put to her at present. The police woman beside him, in charge of Judy's half dried handbag was getting restive. He switched off the recorder, took up the handbag and passed it across the table.

"You'll have to get the passport renewed," he said. "It's suffered rather badly."

"Catch me going away this side of Christmas," she answered defiantly.

In London the news from Devonshire, with particulars reported widely in all the national newspapers, came as a shock to the Haseldyne publishers and to George Carr. The former were more than ever distracted. Their lawyer had not been able to make any sense of the explanations Stockley had given about the plagiarism and now the fellow was dead, so they never would know.

George Carr, on the other hand, chuckled as he read

about Judy Smith's appeal for help and the injured authoress's compassionate response.

"What now?" he asked Ian Macalister on the phone.

"How d'you mean?"

"Looks as if our Anita has made it up with that ambitious and unprincipled hussy. Will you have a compromise on your hands instead of an open and shut court case? The girl's going to get the bulk of the sympathy."

"We don't know who we're dealing with now. No near relatives, apparently. Distant cousins refuse all responsibility over the business. Don't want to know. Been estranged for years."

"Difficult."

"You can say that again."

But a couple of days later another letter from the Stockley side gave a glimmering of light in the otherwise pitch dark prospect. Sir Edgar Seven of the well-known and respected consultant company had undertaken to consider Haseldyne's complaint and wanted to know the details. The dead man's publishing business had been a solo affair and would be wound up. Sir Edgar had helped to finance it and his stake in it could be repaid, as could the other debts. But there was no question of any litigation. He had played the role of benefactor, no more. He understood Miss Armstrong's position; she had his sympathy. He believed the late Mr. Stockley had been more sinned against than sinning. Young people nowadays—

"This Sir Edgar Seven must have his lawyer under his thumb, dictating this rigmarole about juvenile crime," Ian Macalister told the rest of Haseldyne's directors, assembled at the firm's headquarters.

"What's the proposal, if any?" one of them demanded.

"Adequate compensation for the sin of plagiarism, amount unspecified. Remaindering of hardbacks of *The Young Adventurers*. Withdrawal of paperbacks too, in this country, but continued sale of paperbacks abroad, with royalties paid to Anita at current rate, through him, because he would collect them, in English and translation and manage the dispatch and distribution."

"Can we do that?"

"Calls himself a consultant, but I don't doubt he's well in with his exporting and importing clients."

"Will Miss Armstrong play?" another director asked.

"We could try. She does need money. *The Eve of Yesterday* is doing very nicely, but not by any means in the best-seller bracket."

"What about the girl?"

"Knows nothing really, I understand, except how to save her skin."

"Swimming. I take my hat off to her. Good-looker, too."

"They'll make her cough up that prize, won't they?"

Ian dragged back his fellow directors from an intriguing discussion of Judy's attractions and sins, her past and her future, both equally doubtful and therefore fascinating.

But in the end they agreed to instruct their own lawyer to meet Sir Edgar Seven's approach with a limited interest and unlimited caution and to set out the proposals in a simple form that might appeal to Miss Anita Armstrong.

XVIII

An inquest was held in Feltbridge upon the deaths of
Leonard and Clare Stockley of London at sea in the late
afternoon of November 15th, when the pair, man and wife,
had left Dartmouth in a cabin cruiser belonging to Miss
Judith Smith of Plymouth, who was the only survivor of the
accident.

Since the couple had died in the same incident and were
so closely connected, the coroner said, it was thought fitting
to take them together. The little boat had been wrecked on
the bar at the entrance to Salcombe Harbour in heavy
weather, with a strong south-easterly wind and a falling
tide. He would take the medical evidence first to establish
the cause of death.

The pathologist who had performed both post mortems
then produced his facts. Both subjects had died from
drowning. He understood the woman had been picked up
from the sea and did not show any signs of injury beyond
drowning. Nor had she any signs of disease, internal or
external. The man, on the other hand, whose body was
found in the cabin of the wreck, had besides evidence in the
lungs of drowning, sustained a very severe injury to the
head. The back of the skull had been blown off and most of
the brain was missing.

"Did you say *blown off*?" the coroner asked, in a
shocked voice.

"I did. Nothing else would account for the degree of injury sustained."

"Only to the head?"

"The head and neck and those muscles and bones forming the back of the neck."

"*After* death had occurred from drowning?"

"If it had been before he could not have lived to drown."

The coroner's face tightened at the implied rebuke but he said nothing.

The doctor was replaced by Detective Inspector Whimple, who described recovering Judith Smith from Siddicombe, her description of her fall overboard and swim ashore.

"We will go into that with the witness herself," the coroner said and called Judy to the stand.

As near as she could remember, she repeated the description she had given to Whimple of how she came to be in the sea, putting it down to Clare's panic over the weather rather than to a deliberate attack. She kept it vague and was relieved to find the coroner could not keep up with her careful confusion of words. It would pass all right, she hoped, because she wasn't in this place being pinned down by all those needling questions the fuzz had mixed her up in.

She was right. Besides, the coroner, like the police, was more shocked and more deeply curious about that 'explosion' than about this reckless, inexperienced young mariner's lucky escape from death.

He called the insurance assessor next to give his opinion about the hypothetical explosion.

"A very real one if I may say so, sir," the man said.

"I have called you to say so. Explain, please."

Unchastened, but considerate of provincial touchiness, the assessor went into technical detail about the hole in the cruiser's bottom, the damage without and within the vessel, the relatively small charge used, the position chosen for

180

some sort of container, watertight and well cushioned probably, to protect the clock and also prevent its ticking being noticed.

"The position?" asked the coroner.

"In the bilges."

"So this—er—bomb, we may as well call it for convenience, was not in your opinion lethal, unless someone was directly above it in the cabin?"

"As we found someone was, but already dead."

"Just so. My point is that this bomb was really meant just to sink the vessel."

"At sea that would be lethal, sir. In harbour, it might be possible for no one to be on board when it sank."

"Thank you."

At this point Detective Inspector Whimple asked to be recalled. He had just received extra confirmation of the exact time when the cabin cruiser had sunk. The Salcombe resident who had reported the approaching accident was positive there was no explosion before the vessel capsized and sank. Nor was any heard or any disturbance noticed later. It must have taken place after the rescue launch had left the scene with the recovered body of Mrs. Stockley.

The coroner found each of the deaths due to accidental causes. He issued certificates in that sense for each. He also spoke a few words about the dangers to amateurs who elected to go to sea in all weathers, regardless. Miss Smith was no exception. She was not responsible for the holing of her boat, because she, herself, was the only member of the trio on board who knew how to manage the craft and she was clearly not out for suicide. Further police inquiries, he hoped, would discover those responsible for such wickedness.

With this unequivocal result Judy and her father went home, arguing all the way. For, whereas Judy wanted the cabin cruiser declared a total loss and written off with full insurance paid to her, Dad declared the damage on the Salcombe bar was comparatively trivial apart from the hole in the bottom and responsibility for that rested with the bastards who had planted the explosive. The insurance company clearly agreed with his opinion, as witness all the assessor had said at the inquest. They were unlikely to pay up till the villains were found, charged and convicted. Also the boat could be mended, it was by no means a write-off.

For two days Judy continued to argue, but she made no progress. Since Dad had paid the first premium on the insurance to help her over a transaction she did not understand and she had not yet repaid him the amount, she was at a disadvantage in the quarrel, now bitter, between them.

She was becoming desperate. She guessed the probable source of the bomb; she dreaded the consequences to herself of its discovery by the police. Already she knew there were moves to demand from her the return of the book prize money, most of which had gone upon buying the *Adventurer*.

But one piece of news, the significance of which came to her as she sought desperately for help, did suggest that she had it in her hands if she only dared to use it. There was no future for her in Plymouth. There could be one abroad. Some how she must get there. The first attempt had failed. Her basic, total self-interest backed by solid physical courage, did not fail. A week after the inquest she told her parents she was going to London again to spend a few days with her friend, Sylvia.

She took a single suitcase with most of her new smart clothes. She caught an early morning train from Plymouth. She arrived at the City office of Solway, Seven Limited in mid-afternoon and asked for Sir Edgar Seven, giving her name as Julia Trebannon.

Entry was difficult. She had no appointment. She demanded to speak to Sir Edgar's secretary. She heard that Sir Edgar was out and might not be back that day.

"He isn't out," Judy said firmly. "I just saw him come in."

"I'm sorry." The secretary's voice was cold, but less emphatic. "Sir Edgar has no vacant appointment."

"Then he can bloody well switch one," said Judy, losing her temper fast. "And you can tell him so and tell him it's urgent. He knows me and so do you or if you think you don't, you soon will."

The secretary instantly ended this conversation, the receptionist stared at Judy in open-mouthed horror and the girl, seeing this expression, filled the small reception space with her loud and raucous laugh.

A few minutes later the secretary herself appeared, said briefly, "Follow me, please," and led Judy to the door of Sir Edgar's room.

"Go straight in," she said, standing back to make way for the girl, but not announcing her. Judy's temper began to rise again, but she obeyed.

She had not seen Ned since the night of the party at Sunningdale. And her last view of him then had been of a staggering, slipping, awkward, middle-aged bulk with a furious scarlet face, eyes glaring at her as he fell, twisting sideways, into the swimming pool. The figure she now approached across the noise-absorbing office carpet was seated, upright but menacing, and the face was pale and set, the eyes blank and ice-cold.

"Yes?" said Sir Edgar.

Judy took a deep breath. She had planned to confront him with the facts of her failed trip to France. She had expected him to show surprise, perhaps to congratulate her on her escape from drowning. He had done neither. Just asked her business with that single word. All right, he could have it.

"I want help—Ned," she said slowly, carefully, looked about her for a chair, walked over to it and sat down.

His eyes gleamed, but his expression did not change. He

had considered recording this interview as he so often had reproduced his interviews with prospective and actual clients. But he decided that this girl was, as before, unpredictable, so he moved a hand to switch off and repeated his single inquiry with a different word.

"Well?" he said.

It was a little too much for Judy. The strains of all those perils, so unsuited to her real nature, that she had encountered from the very start of her friendship with Chris Trotter, now drove her beyond caution, beyond reason, almost, but not quite, beyond the ultimate disclosure of all she knew of this unforgivable enemy.

She sprang to her feet.

"You old villain!" she shouted at him. "Sitting there pretending you're God Almighty, after what you did to Chris, setting him up and encouraging him in wicked ways, his poor old Auntie Muriel told me who he was, you didn't know that, Ned, did you? And Len, you could twist him round your little finger and I know why, too. Clare told me things you'd never believe, but it all comes back to you. Murderer, that's what you are! You drowned Chris in that pool of yours and you'd of done the same to me if you hadn't been too eager, you effing old bugger, trying to make me drunk, didn't you know I was pouring it away as fast as those guys of yours filled my glass up. And trying to drown us all at sea with a bomb in my boat, my poor little lovely *Adventurer*."

She was out of breath and had to pause to look at her enemy. He had not moved a finger nor altered in any way the frozen look on his face. He simply waited, assessing her words, balancing their true worth with their possible effect. So far they had not implied that she knew anything vital or had any proof to support these allegations. So he did not bother to answer her. He respected her enough not to attempt denial.

Judy understood his attitude, nor was she surprised by it.

The cunning old devil was sharp enough to have got away so far with his off-the-record jobs, mixing them in with his real business. In spite of a cold feeling down her spine as she watched him, she went on with her prepared demand, but in much quieter tones, though still on her feet as if to take sudden flight if that should be necessary.

"I said I wanted help from you, Ned. So I do. You're going to help me, too. I expect you know that already. You've not been too lucky so far, have you? The pigs are on to a lot, you know. Chris for one. He drowned in river water. They know that. They've been looking for where it happened. They know about me being scared off at your so-called party and why."

"How do you know *that*?"

It had burst from him before he could choke it back. He recovered at once, but was now shaking.

"I'm not telling," she answered triumphantly, and went on, "Wouldn't you like to know! You bungled it pretty badly and the next one, meant to finish off all the danger spots, me and Len and Clare in one fell swoop, that mean bomb in the bilges. Well, you picked the wrong weather. No chance of me reaching mid-Channel and us all disappearing, was there, with the wind set in the south-east?"

"How in hell do *you*, of all people, know *that*?"

His anger had melted into sheer astonishment.

"Why not? I've been out fishing with Dad since I was old enough to climb aboard his old boat."

"You are talking nonsense. You told no one you were proposing to go abroad, did you? At the inquest and I suppose before to the police, you are reported to have said you were taking your boat with two friends from Dartmouth to Plymouth."

"And I think you guessed it would be France. I think you knew Len and Clare were going to join me at Dartmouth. I think you had the bomb planted in case and you didn't

185

much care so long as we all drowned. You're a duffer, Ned, aren't you?"

There was silence in the room again. Judy sat down, fighting the exhaustion of her unaccustomed battle of words.

Then Sir Edgar said, "What do you want?"

Judy was ready. She spoke with enormous relief.

"I want you to take me with you to the south of France."

"You *what*?"

Judy explained. He dared not stay in England while the fuzz was looking for the bomb planters. The inquest might be over; their search was not. The Stockleys' London home would be gone over, must have been by now, and very thoroughly. Though nothing had come out at the inquest about his addiction, it would be discovered, if it was not already known to them. Their connection with him and his company and the publishing business would be investigated, as also his home, Meadowside.

"I have had two perfectly satisfactory interviews with Scotland Yard," Sir Edgar told her.

"But you did not explain it all," she replied. "I've written out what I know and left it to Dad to send to Inspector Whimple at Feltbridge unless he gets a card from me from Monte Carlo in a day or two."

"I don't believe there is anything you could tell this inspector that would affect me at all."

"Oh isn't there?" she answered and without hesitation she recited the substance of her threat.

It was enough, but there were difficulties.

"How can you leave the country? Your passport?"

"Found wet, but dried out. Can't use it. You'll have to get me another in another name. You know how, of course."

"What do you propose to travel as? I shall certainly go in my own name. I have no wife or daughter. Will you be niece, mistress, or what?"

"Secretary," said Judy promptly.

"And when is this farce to take place?"

"Tonight. By air."

"You realise that if you are picked up at Heathrow I shall say I engaged you without knowing who you really are, as you were using a false name."

"Then you'd be blowing yourself as well. Dad would be sending my letter to Pig Whimple."

Sir Edgar acknowledged partial defeat. He called in his personal secretary, told Judy to wait in the secretary's office next door and made his arrangements. Sudden business calls were not unusual at Solway, Seven Ltd.

He met Judy at an arranged spot in the air terminal at a given time. They passed separately into the correct departure lounge and from there on to their plane, managing to have adjacent seats. There was no difficulty of any kind. The flight was uneventful. The Monte Carlo hotel welcomed them to a suite overlooking the sea.

Two weeks later Mrs. Grosshouse gave a small party in her cottage at Siddicombe. The Hastons came over from Salcombe, the vicar, his wife and Kate were there. Mrs. Droge stayed late to put the supper dishes on the table in the small dining room and to clear up afterwards.

Nothing remarkable took place during the meal. As Mrs. Droge reported to her friend Phyllis Cook at the post office the next day, you would never have thought anything of it while they were all talking in their quiet posh voices over the meal, putting the plates together at the end of the first course and the gentlemen carrying them out to her. It was later when the excitement began and from then on—

Mrs. Droge was right. The object of the party was to celebrate the successful conclusion of the affair of the plagiarism that had bedevilled Anita Armstrong's new novel.

The Fords at last understood what all the fuss had been

about. Mrs. Ford had to confess that she had enjoyed *The Young Adventurers* though she did not care for some of the modern slang in it: she was sure nobody spoke like that in Edwardian times.

"I expect they did among themselves," Kate insisted. "I mean what used to be called the lower classes did, don't you think?"

"But these weren't supposed to be that, were they?" her mother asked, further confused.

Mervyn came to the rescue.

"No, of course not. You are quite right, Joan. Actually Kate is right, too. That book is a silly, romantic mess. It couldn't be more unlike *The Eve of Yesterday*, could it?"

"No," said the vicar, intervening to save his wife the further embarrassment of confessing that she had not read the true Armstrong novel.

Mrs. Grosshouse explained the terms of the final agreement, which her agent George considered fair. She would have royalties, not the whole, but a fair share, of the paperback editions, English and translation, of *The Young Adventurers*, while the hardbacks, which were mostly library copies, would be remaindered and disappear.

"Have you ever seen the paperback?" Kate asked. "We got the library copy, Mother and I."

Mrs. Grosshouse laughed.

"You'll never believe it, but I actually bought one in Italy, in English, not translated, to read on the plane and never did so until I looked at it at home and saw it was really *my book*—"

Mervyn and Sarah, who had kept this knowledge to themselves, laughed at the vicarage surprise.

"Did you throw it in the dust bin?" Kate asked, smiling.

"Of course not. Sent it to George, my agent. No, I didn't. I must still have it. I'll get it."

It was at this point that the excitement, as Mrs. Droge described it, began.

188

The author searched her shelves, upstairs and downstairs, with no result for some time. Then Mrs. Ford, pulling out one book to look behind it, dislodged another. A bent, twisted object came with it—the missing paperback!

They surrounded Anita as she took the thing in her hand; in fact, snatched it. The paper cover, already loosened, tore sideways. The spine, glued, not sewn, was exposed, the glue cracked and as the author turned the ruin over and back again a small packet fell on the floor.

Mervyn picked it up. He took it to the dining table, demanded scissors and very carefully slit it open. A number of tiny white tablets fell on the polished surface.

"I think," he said to Mrs. Grosshouse, "you would be well advised to ring up that nice Detective Inspector Whimple at Feltbridge and ask him to come over at once."

So the evening ended with that familiar sight a police car, containing this time Whimple, a detective sergeant and a police doctor. A further, closer search was made of the shelf where the paperback had lain hidden for so long.

"It got pushed back," Mrs. Grosshouse protested. "I didn't want it, so I didn't notice it was out of sight. I didn't try to hide it. Why should I?"

"Why indeed," agreed Whimple, thoughtfully.

One more scrap of torn paper was rescued from the floor. It had great significance, since it held an address in code.

The party broke up as soon as the police car had driven away with their prize.

"Those little pills were drugs, weren't they?" Mrs. Ford asked the vicar as they walked home. "Just like the ones my mother had injected before she died."

"Heroin, I expect," Kate said cheerfully. "What a neat way of selling it, if that was what it was there for."

"We shall never really know," the vicar said and sighed for the evil ingenuity of the wicked.

But Mervyn said to Anita, "This puts paid to your paperback agreement, my dear. I hope you haven't signed anything yet."

"I did, and posted the contract this morning with a ninepenny stamp."

"Then you'll have to ring up your agent, George, first thing tomorrow and tell him to cancel it. Who is this man, Seven?"

"A fiend out of hell," said Mrs. Grosshouse with conviction.

But in bed that night, seeing a long programme of work before her, to make up for those lost, unholy paperbacks, she said to herself, "I could strangle that greedy bitch, Judy."

The Law had its facts now, the truth about the failed publishing business, just another attempt to distribute widely, secretly, by means of copies of a popular romance, a small number of shots for addicts together with the source of further supplies. Not all copies held the drug. The drugbearing ones were marked. Very subtle, that. Chris Trotter's work here, in the design on the cover, which was the same as that on the jacket of the hardback. Very neat, just a matter of reverse in the figures. So he had been in it from the start, too. Solway, Seven, Export and Import. Obvious. Lucrative. Very much so.

The truth was plain, too, about the need to dispose of Chris who must, very unwisely, have been trying to blackmail his uncle. Chris, who had lured poor Len Stockley into Uncle Ned's criminal net. The printers of the book, too, perhaps. Or only the book binders? Investigation straightforward, but speed required.

Speed, with the help of Interpol, was applied. It was just over two weeks since young Judy Smith, still hopefully trailed, had left Heathrow for the south of France. They already had the passenger list for that flight; they knew of her connection with Sir Edgar. The French police gave them his present address. Detective Superintendent Knox, with two assistants, one a woman, flew to Monte Carlo.

Sir Edgar Seven received them quietly. He listened to the charges against him of murder, by drowning in the case of Christopher Trotter and the attempted murder by drowning of the two Stockleys and Judith Smith. Also a further charge of drug peddling, using some of the paperback copies of a certain prize novel by the girl, calling herself Julia Trebannon. Where was she now?

"In America," Sir Edgar told them. "She left me at the end of my first week here, with a young American tourist who appeared to have plenty of money. I know his name; he was on a travel tour. You may be able to find him. And her. A good-looking girl and about as reliable as a scorpion. Her present passport is in the name of Edna Baynes."

"As a matter of interest," Knox asked. "Why did you up and run? Weren't you sitting pretty?"

"Very pretty. But she knew about the books. I didn't, of course. She guessed why Len had taken so many with him when he flitted. He needed them for his addiction. She guessed that."

"You knew of his addiction, then?"

"All his friends did. She knew about the books. I repeat, I knew nothing. But she threatened me, so I gave in to her and brought her here."

"You can tell all that to your counsel, Sir Edgar. Shall we go," Knox said.

Judy Smith was traced to the young American's home in Colorado, but she had already moved on. Neither he nor his friends knew where, or they had a shrewd guess, but were not saying.

Later Mr. Smith had a postcard from Mexico. But by that time he had sent her letter to Detective Inspector Whimple. It only confirmed Sir Edgar's suggestion about her guess regarding the heroin in the paperbacks. It was noted on her

191

file and disregarded, as Sir Edgar had been put away for life with a minimum on the drugs charge of fifteen years. Others in his confidence and in his pay were exposed in due course. It took time, but Knox was keen.

A few years after this the gossip papers had pictures of a very lovely girl, who had won a beauty prize in a South American state. It was recognised by her parents and friends and everyone who remembered her former appearance in these papers. It was Judy Smith, known now as Carlotta Anglicana, as beautiful as ever, smiling and very, very confident.